LUNA

RICK CHESLER

SEVERED PRESS
HOBART TASMANIA

LUNA

ISBN: 978-1-925342-69-7

ACKNOWLEDGEMENTS

The author thanks Doug Corleone for his insightful input into the
early drafts of this novel.

Thanks also to Gary Lucas and Severed Press for helping this story
to see the light of day.

PROLOGUE | RABBIT HOLE

Every laborious step astronaut Strat Knowles took caused him to flash on the blown-up photograph of Buzz Aldrin that had stood at the far edge of his cluttered desk since his second year of high school. The photo had been snapped by Neil Armstrong during the first moon landing on July 20, 1969, long before Strat was even born, yet it seemed as though he'd lived in that singular moment more than any other over the past fifteen years. As a teenager, he'd spent countless hours imagining what it would be like to walk on the moon, whether it would be, as astronauts past had described, like plodding through water. He'd practiced walking along the bottom of his parent's pool to see what it what feel like.

Strat no longer had to imagine.

The awe he'd long ago conceived remained with him as he approached the entrance to the underground warren into which his colleague had descended twenty-six minutes ago, yet it was accompanied by a fear he'd never fathomed. Jayson had entered the tunnels in search of a third colleague, Grant, who was due back to the surface more than an hour ago. Both of Strat's colleagues had gone silent, leaving nothing behind but the static currently swelling within his helmet. Strat was alone in the icy realm of the moon's subterranean spaces, and now his only available course of action was to follow Grant and Jayson down the rabbit hole.

Strat couldn't alone operate the spacecraft meant to bring them home, nor could he simply lift the radio receiver and summon help. No one could reach him in time. It was like being alone in the Death Zone on Everest. The only chance of survival was heading down, even as his body threatened to freeze where he stood.

He spoke into his transmitter once more but could barely hear his own words through all the static. He started his descent.

It took longer than the seven minutes it should have, his instincts forcing his fingers to tighten around the safety rope every twenty seconds or so. It was still strange to push downward in the low gravity. Even if he survived and made a dozen more trips to the moon, he'd never grow used to it.

If.

It was the first time Strat recognized that he might never again see Earth.

One last glimpse.

Why hadn't he bothered to steal one last glimpse? Because in all his years of fanaticizing, he'd never once imagined perishing on the moon itself, only on the journey. He'd seen footage of the Space Shuttle *Challenger* breaking apart seventy-three seconds after the launch of its tenth mission, exploding into a massive ball of flames. As a child in 2003, he'd been glued to the television and witnessed the disintegration of *Columbia* as the space shuttle re-entered Earth's atmosphere. Since then, there had been no catastrophic disasters. Not a single fatality. More than a decade ago, space travel entered the private sector and now it was said to be as safe as speeding down a dark and twisting freeway while mildly intoxicated. An acceptable risk for stepping into another world.

Still, Strat had ensured his affairs were in order before the launch. He knew the dangers. But the hazards lie in the equipment that sent the crew from Earth to the moon and back. Not on Luna's surface. And certainly not below it.

Humanity was about to enter the age of space tourism. This, as far as Strat knew, was one of the last missions to the moon not carrying paying passengers. Those back on Earth who had placed deposits to reserve seats upwards of $25 million were waiting, counting the days to their scheduled launch in less than a year.

Strat's right foot touched solid ground and he shoved himself away from the wall. In his ears, the static continued, a sound so irritating it may as well have been inside his head. He weighed the option of shutting the radio off, possibly missing a message from Grant or Jayson, against keeping it on and moving forward amidst the distracting cacophony. His temper flaring, he abruptly turned the sound off.

Silence. Blessed silence as thick as the walls on either side of him.

Strat guided his light down the tunnel immediately in front of him. This was where Grant was four minutes before they lost contact. This was the tunnel his crewmate had announced he was entering.

Copy that, Strat had told him, voice steeped with the dullness of routine.

He kicked his left foot forward, followed with his right, picturing good ol' Buzz moonwalking atop his desk back on Earth.

You're on the bottom of Pop's pool, Strat told himself. *You can do this.*

He remained entirely conscious of the passing time. Jayson had remained in contact for a few minutes longer than Grant, so it wasn't as though there was a spot in this tunnel that had simply gobbled them up. Here on the moon, everyone moved at precisely the same slow, deliberate pace, a pace dictated by the low gravity.

As the third minute passed, Strat for the first time wondered why the hell they'd had to explore these and the other underground tunnels in the first place. But he knew the reason, he just happened to disagree with it. They were meant to map out a safe route for ticket-holders; the CEO of Outer Limits, the company Strat worked for, was concerned that folks wanted more for their twenty-five mil than a mere stroll on the moon's surface.

As if these tunnels are going to get asses in the seats. It's the view they're paying for, to stand on another planetary body and see the famed Earthrise with one's own eyes...priceless. Who needs this crap down here?

There had been talk of something else, but only among the directors. Some sort of attraction, Strat figured. Over the next decade, Outer Limits' founder Blake Garner had plans for a moon base, a few permanent, manned stations. Ultimately, Strat was certain, he'd put in an amusement park. After all, the man worshipped Walt Disney, wanted to do for the moon what Disney had done for theme parks back on Earth—to make it a must see destination, a fun-filled adventure for the whole family—as long as they could, and would, pay.

And it would probably work, Strat mused. Space tourism would take off. *No pun intended.* Eventually, the moon would be colonized, and Blake Garner and his company would remain at the center of everything, a Google or Apple for the business of space, a Disney for the Space Generation masses.

Strat's eyes flicked to the right as a puff of dust seemed to emanate from the wall. He turned and pressed himself against the rock on the opposite side and fixed the spot with his gaze. The wall seemed to shift and Strat was suddenly certain he was seeing things. Not a good sign even on Earth, but a far more dangerous thing on the moon.

He checked the gauges on his display module, but nothing seemed to be malfunctioning. He still had ample oxygen flowing.

Yet the wall moved again. Somehow, it seemed to be *opening*.

Before he could kick a single foot back in the direction from which he'd come, the rock swiftly vanished before his eyes, replaced instantly by an abominable and perfectly unrecognizable image. He squeezed shut his eyes, and within the absolute soundlessness of the helmet that had thus far kept him alive, Stratford Knowles parted his lips in a scream.

1 | SOMEBODY'S GOTTA DO IT

An aging man stood at the dawn of what everyone around these parts, and quite a few beyond, hoped would usher in a new era: Spaceport America, New Mexico. Risen from the arid ground in a gush of post-dot-com era dollars and heady X-Prize enthusiasm, what would otherwise be one of the most desolate parts of the U.S. was now making a very real bid to take the entire country straight back to the future via private spacecraft.

The man, still physically fit despite his years, wore a plastic badge on a lanyard around his neck and clutched a boxy, battered briefcase so long out of style he was occasionally offered cash for it on the street by some retro-chic hipster. He shaded his eyes from the glaring sun as he stared at the complex of glassy, ultra-modern buildings spread out before him. Some distance away from them, a gleaming, white rocket waited on a launch pad, supported by towering scaffolding. He shook his head full of thick, graying hair at the improbability of it all and began walking toward the largest building, wherein he knew his reputation preceded him.

Nobody liked Federal Aviation Administration Safety Inspector James Burton. Except for the people who flew on the planes he inspected. They sure would like him, if they even knew he existed. But they don't ever see him. It's the pilots and mechanics and airline administrators who see him. And they don't like him. He's used to that, though. It's his job to point out when they're screwing up, and to let their bosses know about it. He was thorough enough that he'd been chosen to represent the FAA on a clearance flight for one of two private companies in a highly publicized and well-funded race to conduct the first tourist moon landing.

His stint in the Air Force hadn't hurt either, he supposed. He'd even been to space once, technically, that is, if one wasn't too picky about where the Earth's atmosphere stopped and "space" began—in a jet. For a few seconds at Mach 2.6, he'd looked up and seen that eerie black sky at high noon over California. And it was those few seconds' worth of "space experience" that had vaulted him above his fellow civil service drones who wouldn't know a negative-g dive if it bit them in the ass.

Still, he figured his role here was more symbolic than functional. After all, he'd only been in space for about five seconds in that Air Force jet, all those decades ago, and that was in the co-pilot seat at that. It was like picking a candidate to visit the Mariana Trench in a submarine based on the fact that he'd once stuck his toe in the water at the beach, while everyone else lived in Kansas. Besides, everybody knew that the real space experts—qualified aeronautics engineers—had already checked these craft out, and they were good to go. Been up a dozen times already with the commercial astronauts. They had it down.

Now these two civilian outfits were each one round-trip lunar flight away from being granted clearance to take any Joe Blow with more money than sense to the moon. So why not make it his swan song to help things along, to put the stamp of America's premier air transportation safety agency on this exciting new form of travel? To get to space, one had to travel through the air, after all.

He was due to retire in six more weeks, however, but this would really give him something to go out on, wouldn't it? *Burton was the man!* he could hear his colleagues saying after he'd left, no longer a denizen of those stale cubicle farms full of filing cabinets older than he was and grungy, crowded break rooms. All he had to do was strap himself in for the ride, put himself in the shoes of a paying passenger, make sure the crews explained the safety precautions well enough for him to understand and convey to others, and that would be it.

Yet the truth was he didn't really want to go. Retirement was a few weeks away. Wife. Vacation house. Kids, grandkids. He had a lot to live for. What else did he need? His pension was secure regardless of whether he accepted this assignment. But for some reason when they'd asked him to do it, he couldn't turn it down. Pride, maybe. Or stupidity. Something. Whatever it was, it had led him, right here, right now, to a commercial rocket on a launch pad in Spaceport America, New Mexico, bound for the *moon*. Yet, as he approached the entrance to the largest building, he knew exactly why he'd opted to go.

Stenson. Pete Stenson. *He might have had something to do with it, right? That pompous bastard.* Burton shoved aside thoughts of his former boss at the FAA. Stenson was the government ride-along on the other flight. That company was owned by the dot-com billionaire who made that search engine everyone uses, while Burton was assigned to the one bankrolled by the guy who founded some online payment system. Yippee for that guy. But apparently making billions in e-commerce wasn't enough; he had sufficient drive and ambition left over to personally start his own space company and quite literally shoot for the moon. It was enough to make Burton's own aspirations for a quiet retirement where an adventurous day would see him in a rowboat catching bass on a lake look ridiculously quaint by comparison.

James reached for the double glass doors and was surprised to see them automatically swing open. He withdrew his hand, semi-embarrassed, and strode into the high-ceilinged lobby. A pretty, headset-wearing receptionist in her mid-twenties glanced at his badge and gave him a room number where, apparently, "They can't wait to meet you!" He thanked her and took one of the cars at the elevator bank to the sixth and top floor.

He exited the elevator and walked down a plush carpeted hallway featuring framed photographs of various spacecraft, as well as various celebrities, over the decades. One of them depicted Blake Garner, the owner of the spaceship James was getting ready to ride on, shaking hands with President George W. Bush on the steps of the White House. Another had Blake on stage with a famous rock band, introducing the act with his arm around the lead singer in front of a capacity crowd in some arena that bore his company's name.

Nearing the end of the hall, James checked the room numbers, opened one and stepped inside.

2 | SHIPMATES

"Mr. Burton, it's a pleasure to welcome you to Outer Limits!" Blake Garner's ebullient facade greeted James as he stepped inside the room. Other than the space entrepreneur, there was no one else in here. James found this odd since the purpose of his visit was to meet the rest of the team he'd be sharing the spaceship with. Sharing the moon with, he reminded himself.

Blake wrapped his arms around the FAA man who ducked back in surprise. It wasn't a typical greeting for a federal employee, and the two did not even know each other. James hoped Blake wasn't drinking or worse, but realized he was probably just high on excitement, or more accurately, as was often the case, he was high on himself.

And why shouldn't he be? Blake Garner was about to lead humankind into a new and exhilarating era, was about to launch what would likely be the most important industry since computers. Well, that's not entirely accurate, though, is it? James thought to himself. Because while Blake was certainly a pioneer, he wasn't the only one in the running. In fact, Blake's primary competitor in the race to bring the moon to the common man (or at least the rich one), was already in space, probably even on the lunar surface as they spoke.

James knew that this competition of sorts was something that made Blake extremely nervous—his arch-rival, Kennedy Haig, founder and CEO of Black Sky, L.L.C., had what amounted to at least a three-day head-start to obtaining clearance to take the first paying passengers. And with all seats on the first lunar flight, should it be green-lighted, already booked and paid for—for both companies—Blake knew full well that a three-day head start was all one of them needed to be crowned the winner in the space-experience-buying public's eyes. Sure, there was room for more than one player, but to be the first mover represented enormous intangible benefits.

Critics of both Blake and Kennedy charged that space tourism would be a fad, something that would fade with time like online social networks or drive-in movies. But the feeling was that there were more true believers than skeptics. After all, the market had clearly spoken, the stock prices for both space companies shooting for the stars in lockstep with their actual efforts. Analysts had continuously pushed the predicted date back, from 2025 a few years ago, to 2030 as recently as last year. Yet here it was, 2024, with the market showing no signs of shedding its upward momentum.

Blake Garner, estimated net worth of $12.7 billion, beckoned for James to follow him back into his private oval-shaped office, which could have easily been mistaken for a wing at Hayden Planetarium. Well-above their heads, a dome-shaped projection screen created a night sky, alive with slow-moving stars and planets, with the occasional comet or asteroid sweeping across the blackness.

James looked toward the curved walls for light fixtures but saw none. A pair of lamps sitting on opposite ends of his polished black desk illuminated a small section of the office like headlights. James waited for his eyes to adjust to the dark, hoping he wouldn't need to take any notes in here. He could probably peck one out on his smartphone, but he disliked using that thing for anything more than making phone calls.

"What do you think?" Blake said, motioning around the absurd room.

The question struck James as odd, the words of a man plagued by terrible insecurity.

"Extraordinary." It certainly beat the hell out of the government offices he'd worked in the last few decades, that was for sure. Then again, he wasn't sure how much real work he could do in a place like this. Seemed more like some kind of fancy den or high-tech man cave. But when you had thirteen billion to your name, James supposed you could call your office whatever the hell room you wanted.

Blake motioned to a black leather chair across from his desk while he rounded the monstrous slab of furniture and took a seat. He moved like a man half his age. Not quite fifty, Garner was a self-proclaimed adrenaline junkie. When he wasn't scuba diving Australia's Great Barrier Reef or climbing mountains in the Himalayas, he could usually be found jumping off buildings or out of planes. At least that was how the media portrayed him. And for all his feigned modesty, he didn't seem to mind. His piercing blue seemed to sparkle with energy as he spoke.

"So, I understand the training went remarkably well!" There was that unwavering enthusiasm again. James recognized that it could be infectious, and it even seemed genuine, but he found it to be almost tiresome, like that guy at a party who needs to take it down a notch. Except for Blake, that party never ended.

Not only that, James mused, but Blake said it as though he'd taken a forty-hour bartending course, not just returned from Moscow following seven straight days of intensive space training, just as the first space tourists would pay for the privilege to do. James couldn't see why. It was a fairly grueling mish-mash of classroom lectures, spacecraft simulator exercises, and physical fitness training. Personally, he had found none of it particularly vexing when taken individually, but as a whole, and combined with the Russian travel, it was certainly taxing. And now the real test was about to start.

James was about to tell him how it had gone well, no problems, thanks, when a voice made to sound as though it had to travel millions of vertical miles suddenly broke through a speaker on Blake's desk.

"Sir, Martin Hughes to see you."

"Thank you, dear. Please escort him back."

James' interest crept up a notch. Martin Hughes was a star, at least insofar as scientists could be stars. A world-renowned atheist, though he referred to himself as a "secular naturalist," Hughes was at the very top of his game. He'd written several international bestsellers on topics in the field of astrobiology, but also on philosophy, free thought and the fact that we no longer needed an idea such as god to explain the "miracles" of our natural universe. His was an interesting voice, but James couldn't help but wonder if Blake had chosen him for the mission precisely because his very presence would be so controversial. The more controversy, the more media time. Blake was no stranger to this concept.

"Martin!" Blake jumped out of his chair and extended his arms for an embrace, one James noticed that Martin returned without reservation. "Wonderful to see you." Martin was a large man, though not overweight, but he was taller than both Blake and James. His bald head reflected the planetarium light from the ceiling.

James stood in greeting.

"Martin, I'd like you to meet my government watchdog."

James frowned, but he had to give the man points for his directness. It was basically true.

Hughes stood stock-still, scrutinizing James' face before saying, "Well-trained watchdog, I hope?"

An awkward silence hung in the room while Blake and Martin waited for James' reaction. Finally, Hughes laughed. Blake joined him. The sound created a strange, awful echo in the colossal room.

"Kidding, my dear boy," Hughes said in his thick British accent. "I had to summon something droll for our first meeting lest I come off like some haughty old Englishman."

You do anyway, James thought but refrained from saying. He was not afraid of offending anyone, but if he was to travel to the moon (and hopefully back) with these people, then he wanted to make damn sure they got along as well as possible. No need to incite anyone over some silly perceived slight.

Martin dismissed any further comment with a wave of his hand and sat in one of the large black leather seats. Blake and James also reassumed their seated positions.

The two men looked at James, both waiting for him to speak. The meeting, he suddenly realized, was primarily for his benefit. Rather, the FAA's benefit. Strike that – for the benefit of all civilian space travelers.

"So," James began, "what exactly is your interest in this expedition, Mr. Hughes?" It seemed like a non-threatening enough ice-breaker, a softball for the celebrity atheist. James expected a lengthy diatribe on the importance of space exploration to the progress of humankind, but he didn't receive it. Instead, all Martin said was, "Life."

"Life?" James glared at Blake. What the hell was he talking about? They all needed to understand each other perfectly, this was no time to wax poetic, or philosophical. *Because surely he didn't mean—*

"The meaning and significance of life," Blake cut in, giving Martin a hard stare. "Man's place in the universe—are we alone in the cosmos, and all that. Martin, here, expresses such thoughts much more eloquently than myself, but that's about the gist of it, right old chap?"

Martin tipped his head slightly to one side and eyed first James, then Blake. "That's right. And to make myself as open as possible to channeling those eloquent thoughts, I think it's time I turn in early. Just wanted to stop by and meet the watchdog, as it were."

Martin stood, shot James a sly smile and then exited the room.

3 | CELESTIAL BODY

Moments after Martin Hughes exited stage left, Blake told James there was someone else he wanted him to meet prior to Launch Day. James retook his seat and watched as Blake played with the buttons on his control panel.

"Ready," he informed his receptionist.

James swiveled his chair toward the door but it didn't glide open. Instead, a panel in the wall behind him swooshed to one side, revealing a ridiculously large monitor, every bit as mammoth as a movie screen. Blake ran his fingers over a few buttons until an image of a rock face appeared. Then an individual stepped in front of it, and James automatically rose to his feet.

Blake said, "Mr. Burton, I'd like you to meet Asami Imura, PhD, our selenologist."

She was stunning. Dressed in red athletic gear emphasizing every curve, Asami stood facing the camera, her big bright intelligent brown eyes staring at the camera like pools of scalding hot coffee. Wavy black hair cascaded over her shoulders.

"Pleasure to meet you, Mr. Burton. Or might it be Dr. Burton?" She practically sung the words.

"No, just mister." Burton had a bachelor's degree in business administration. He wasn't particularly proud of it, but it had been enough to land him a steady job at the FAA, one he'd kept for his entire career, and that was a rare enough thing these days.

"James is our FAA rep who will be riding along to the moon," Blake informed her.

Riding along, huh? Although James had told himself that's exactly what he'd be doing, somehow coming from Blake it had an offensive ring to it, like he was merely dead weight, nothing more than a rubber stamp to be taken into space and back so they could carry on with their business. But he remained silent, admiring the woman's sleek form on the rock wall.

Blake said, "Catch you in the middle of a climb, did we, Asami?"

"Oh, it's beautiful today, Blake. You should be here."

"I'd love to be." Blake studied the background. "Looks like you're at West Blue Mountain again."

"Right, my fave spot," Asami said.

West Blue was the highest peak in the San Mateo Mountains in the southwestern part of New Mexico. The southern half of the range was extremely difficult to get to, so traffic in the area was always light. Asami appeared to be alone.

"We won't keep you," Blake said to the screen. "Just wanted to make introductions."

Asami clipped a rope to a carabiner and then eyed the camera. "I look forward to the launch, gentlemen."

"As do we."

Just like that, Asami blinked off the screen.

Blake turned to James and winked. "Wanted you to get an eyeful before she dons that unflattering spacesuit."

James forced a conspiratorial grin, wondering how many of the sexual allegations Blake faced throughout his meteoric rise were true. A good number, he was sure. Yet somehow his tawdriness seemed to complement his public image: the poor billionaire playboy lost in a constant search for true love.

The FAA man addressed Blake. "Dr. Imura works for you?"

Garner shook his head. "No, our VP of Marketing – whom you'll be meeting soon – brought her aboard in order for Dr. Imura to offer her *independent* critique of our little travel operation. Quotes from an expert for the promotional materials, the website, brochures, television spots. Dr. Imura is formerly with NASA, which of course means she's studied the moon her entire adult life having never gone into space. So she's very enthusiastic to work with us."

James nodded.

Blake barely hid his disgust as he segued into his next topic. He grimaced and cleared his throat as he hunted for something on his desk. "So, *James*, can I call you Jim? Like a cigar?" Blake slid open a drawer and held out a Cuban. The gesture was a minor one coming from a billionaire, but the implication was both clear and dangerous. Would a government official accept a gift from the owner of a company he was here to regulate?

"No thank you, and James is fine." Burton was no stranger to these kinds of offerings, the ones that were small enough to pass off as an oversight ("It's the same polite gesture that I would afford to anyone I'm about to start working with"), if they were called out on it. He always turned them down, even though he knew that plenty of his colleagues did not. Everybody had a line somewhere, and for many, small tokens of appreciation such as cigars were not on the wrong side of it. But not for James. His whole career he'd played it clean and he wasn't about to change that now, only weeks from retiring.

Blake frowned and stuck the cigar back in the drawer, sliding it shut with a *snap*. "Look, *Mr. Burton*, thus far Outer Limits has always had a good working relationship with the FAA..."

James nodded. This much was true. Blake continued.

"But up to this point we've been working with your superior, Guy Patton." Blake paused to watch James bristle at the word "superior." The unspoken question was, *Why you?*

"Patton was chosen early on to join you," James explained, "but six months ago we were informed he didn't pass the physical. Vision problems. So now you're stuck with me."

After a lengthy pause during which he stared at James, Blake continued. "Anyway, I'll be blunt. We tried to get Pete Stenson but he'd already been roped aboard Black Sky's flight. You have a reputation for being a real stickler for details, even for a government bulldog."

Damn that Stenson. James had little doubt that had he been in his place, Stenson would be smoking that cigar right now, probably toasting Blake with his fine liquor over there in the ivory-accented cabinet. But Stenson wasn't here. He was already on the moon with Black Sky, doing his own job the way he saw fit to do it. And there was nothing James could do about that. Nothing except do *his* job the way he saw fit.

He shrugged, his attitude unapologetic. "I do my job to the best of my abilities. I keep people safe. When a citizen steps onto a commercial airliner, they assume it's safe to do so. They have no way to really verify that for themselves, and they don't know about the processes that go into making it safe, and they don't care. The price of a ticket is supposed to have safety built into it. In the same fashion, when they step onto a spacecraft, including one of yours, they're going to assume it's as safe as it can possibly be. And the small role I have in that process is one I take very seriously."

"I assure you that Outer Limits takes it very seriously as well. After all, I myself will be going on not only this trip, but the first tourist lunar landing also."

"Mr. Garner," James began as he opened a spiral bound notebook, "this will be our final meeting before the launch. Allow me to confirm: Five passengers, including you, me, Dr. Hughes, Dr. Imura, your VP of Marketing—Suzette Calderon, right?—plus your three professional astronauts for a total onboard count of eight."

"Correct. Mr. Burton, may I ask you a question?"

"Please do." James held his pen poised above the notebook. Blake met his gaze.

"Are you frightened?" James rolled his eyes as he let his pen rest.

"Of course, somewhat. Who wouldn't be?"

"Good. Fear's important. It's what keeps us alert to danger. If you don't feel fear, you're either a god or a sociopath."

James stared at him, the image of calmness. "I assume, then, you're experiencing a great deal of fear as well. Although you have been up there before."

Blake smiled, rubbed at the heavy scruff on his right cheek. "Me? No, I don't experience fear. Not like that anyway, not the kind we're talking about."

In James' head, he dismissed this as sheer bravado. Blake was creating an indelible image of himself for the media. Still, he had to wonder just what kind of vision the entrepreneur had for himself, how he wanted to be portrayed.

"What are you then? A sociopath or a god?"

Blake grinned, his eyes genuinely alight for the first time that day. "Well, James, I'm afraid you'll just have to wait for this mission to play out."

"What, no hints?"

Blake shrugged. "Let's just say that I'm not sure the two are mutually exclusive, and leave it at that for the time being."

4 | ROCKET MAN

James arrived an hour before he was told he had to be there on the day of the launch. He stood in the parking lot, taking in the scene, quietly meditating. The sky over New Mexico's Jornada del Muerto basin was so clear he could almost see himself in it. Gazing skyward, the FAA man spotted not a single cloud waiting for its moment to sneak past the sun and drop a bit of rain to delay the launch. He admitted to himself that he could have used an extra day or two. Cold feet in the hot desert, butterflies battling for pole position in the pit of his stomach. More than a few times he thought: *I wonder if Pete Stenson felt this way? If he still feels that way, right now up there on the moon? And Blake, the first time he went up?*

Martin Hughes was next to arrive, and it both comforted and frightened James to learn that this brilliant man was every bit as terrified as he was. Knowing Martin was perhaps the least superstitious man on the planet, James felt at liberty to speak his fears aloud.

"I don't know what it is," he told him, "just this gut feeling that something crucial won't go as planned. I've read too many airliner crash reports, I guess."

The famous atheist didn't say anything, merely continued staring into the blue over the Spaceport.

Awkwardly, James said, "I take it your gut didn't relay the same message to you?"

"Oh, I don't listen to my gut, Mr. Burton. It does nothing but growl. And I sure as hell don't let my gut *think* for me, I'll tell you that."

While they waited, James surveyed the grounds upon which the spaceport was built, nearly thirty square miles which were considered part of the southwest state's Land of Enchantment. Blake Garner, as well as a consortium of other space business interests, had reached an agreement with New Mexico's governor some seventeen years ago, a deal which ultimately provided more than three hundred million dollars of taxpayer money for use in constructing the spaceport.

James and Martin watched the road for the arrival of Blake Garner, but they heard his approach before they saw it. The sound fractured the silence of the pale blue sky with such violence that it startled James.

Martin grinned at him. "You think that's loud, wait until you hear the launch."

Blake's helicopter descended as rapidly as it had appeared. By the time it touched ground, the force of the rotor wash was so strong he feared it would knock him down.

When the 'copter door opened, he expected to see Blake first, as he'd seen him so many times on television, blowing out of the machine and waving, much like the President of the United States when Marine One set down in the Rose Garden.

But today it was a female who first stepped onto the helipad. A beautiful female with features he immediately recognized. As she came toward them, Dr. Asami Imura smiled at the two men standing there.

Next off the 'copter was Blake Garner, his ubiquitous smile replaced by a severe scowl James would witness often in the days to come. Blake skipped the pleasantries; in fact, skipped James and Martin altogether, walking briskly straight for the Spaceport instead.

A casual shrug of the shoulders from Hughes convinced James to follow. Minutes later, they walked silently through a cavernous hangar, then stepped out onto a platform with a full view of the launch pad.

It was the first time James had seen the craft firsthand, and despite the critical detachment from the operation he did his best to maintain, he had trouble suppressing his emotion. He was truly standing at the dawn of a new era for mankind.

The custom Boeing looked as futuristic today as it did a decade ago when Blake's fledgling company first introduced 3D renderings to the public. Standing vertically, its nose aimed straight at the sky, the spacecraft appeared more like a missile than a shuttle.

On its hull, the words *Outer Limits* screamed to be read and respected. Only then did it finally hit James that no matter what happened today or in the days to follow, he was about to make history. Unless, that is, the Black Sky mission succeeded first. Then he supposed he'd be relegated to a footnote of history, a passenger on the Number Two outfit to take people who were not professional astronauts to the moon.

But the notion awakened something inside Burton he barely dared to acknowledge. Was he secretly rooting for Outer Limits to beat Black Sky because he, James Burton, lowly FAA administrator, would make more of a name for himself? Forget cigars and quality liquor, even high-priced call girls—all of which had been thrown his way at one time or another in the line of duty. Immortality...going down in history. He had to admit, it was downright intoxicating to think that he could be remembered— really *remembered*—outside of some dusty protocol files buried deep within the FAA's offices.

Then Blake Garner was waving an arm for everyone to follow him inside, and James strode into the building on his way to the moon.

Another day at the office, right?

5 | COUNTDOWN

"T-minus thirty minutes and counting…" A synthesized female voice with a soothing tonal quality echoed around the spaceport and through the network of communications channels radiating from the Flight Control building like so many nerves from a brain.

Inside the spaceship, Command Module Pilot Caitlin Swain adjusted her headset as she heard the voice and glanced at a small video monitor set into a control panel above her head. A small woman with a head of thick, black curly hair, she cracked a crooked smile before turning to her two fellow crew members seated in the cramped Control Deck of the capsule they occupied atop the massive rocket.

"Here come our passengers. Is it just me or does it look like Blake has his hand on Imura's ass?"

The two men sharing the crew space with Caitlin snickered as they glanced at a different monitor closer to them, showing the same view as Caitlin's. On the tiny screen, Blake held his free hand out in a thumbs-up gesture while he grinned up at the closed-circuit camera. Besides Imura, Caitlin could see that he was phalanxed by the other four passengers who kept their eyes straight ahead as they walked the plank, as it was known—down the hall onto the elevator that would take them to the top of the rocket—the famous exobiologist, Blake's marketing guru, the renowned selenologist, and, *ugh*—the FAA drone.

"She probably can't feel that through her spacesuit," Paul Abbott, the mission's Commander, quipped as he flipped some switches.

"We could have Flight pipe in her heart rate data, see if it did anything for her." Dallas Pace was a thirty-four year-old African

American who served as their Lunar Module Pilot as well as the flight's medical doctor.

Caitlin appreciated the moment of levity. Although they were highly trained for this mission with decades of combined experience between them, she was well aware of the ever-present litany of Things That Could Go Wrong. The takeoff, the lunar landing, Earth reentry. And not just in space either, she reflected. She'd reviewed the Russian flight in the 1960s that made history as the first-ever spacewalk. The spacewalk itself had gone great. But upon return to Earth, the craft had landed off course in a densely forested mountain region and the two cosmonauts had been forced to spend a night in the freezing wilderness, fending off wolves until their ground crew could get to them. Then there was the Apollo splashdown where the capsule hatch had blown prematurely and the capsule almost sank in the ocean, taking an astronaut with it. You just weren't safe until you were all the way back home.

All three of the crew were ex-NASA, members of the ever-growing Astronauts-Who've-Never-Been-to-Space club the agency seemed to cultivate thus far in the 21st century. They'd each made the personal giant leap to the private space industry in the hopes of seeing the fabled black sky through a window instead of on a screen in their professional lifetimes. With Outer Limits, and definitely with Black Sky, it seemed they'd hit the jackpot. *The moon.* Mars was also a target, but so far, too far away into the future. The moon was doable right here, right now.

Caitlin turned to her associates. "Well, boys, after this trip we're space virgins no more."

Paul clicked a dial through various positions while staring at a digital readout. "You know what they say," he said without looking up from what he was doing. "You never forget your first time."

A new voice crackled through the communication loops, that of a throat clearing. "Ahem, gentlemen and *lady*, let's stay focused here, okay?" Ray McCullough, one of a half-dozen Flight Controllers, spoke to them from behind the blue mirrored glass of the Flight Control Building a hundred yards away. Caitlin flashed on last night at *Dos Pueblos* as she matched Ray's scruffy face with the voice, ensconced in the cactus-shrouded back patio at a table for two over plates of enchiladas and prickly pear margaritas, the evening air still 100 degrees, her emotions even hotter.

She keyed her transmitter. "Copy that, Ray, all systems nominal, monitoring countdown, passengers boarding. Command Module standing by, over."

Caitlin saw an indicator light blink on in front of her. She watched as the capsule door slid open below them and Blake Garner stepped into the passenger bay followed by his handpicked team. Well, handpicked except for James Burton, that is. One by one they crossed over the threshold. Burton in particular seemed a little freaked out.

Meanwhile, the artificial voice continued her emotionally flat countdown.

6 | LIFTOFF

Caitlin Swain finished running through yet another checklist and turned to look down on the passenger bay as The Voice told her it was T-minus five minutes. The six passengers had taken their respective launch stations but presently an argument —maybe that was too strong a word — but a *disagreement* of some sort had been building between Blake and his Marketing VP, Suzette Calderon. Caitlin had worked with Suzette before for numerous Outer Limits promotional productions, and knew that the woman was a fiery Latina who insisted on getting her way – and that Blake was used to giving it to her.

There wasn't a lot of small talk. The rest of the passengers seemed preoccupied with triple-checking their launch seat harnesses while Blake pointed an accusatory finger Suzette's way. "I'm not blind. That camera doesn't fit into the restraint, it's too large. That's not the one we spec'd out."

Suzette shrugged. "It's a bit bigger, but it has way more megapixels, so it's entirely worth it." With some effort, she snapped the device into a bulkhead recess and settled back into her seat, apparently satisfied.

Caitlin tuned out the conversation before she had the chance to hear Blake acquiesce as she knew he would. She did a final visual sweep of the passenger bay before her attention would be consumed completely by the control panels that surrounded her. James Burton was the last of them to stop obsessing over his restraint harness and now he fixated on Blake's interaction with Suzette.

Martin Hughes gazed blankly at the wall, completely content. She had no idea how the hell he remained so tranquil. It wasn't drugs, she knew; all eight of them had been subjected to the mandatory testing this morning. Forging out into the cosmos, she supposed. It wasn't just a look of serenity. Hughes seemed to be positively beaming due to some kind of inner peace.

Meanwhile, the FAA man frowned as he watched the Blake-Suzette exchange and wrote something down in a small notepad. He'd been told that, as with commercial airline flights, no electronic devices of any kind would be permitted during sensitive operations like takeoffs and landings. Caitlin agreed with this, but at the same time she thought it was Blake's way of limiting the FAA's in-flight record-keeping capabilities. She agreed with that, too. Especially when it came to Burton, she thought, watching him underline something he wrote with a flourish.

And then it was time.

"...*minus twenty, nineteen, eighteen...*"

Caitlin willed the butterflies from her stomach, the "*this-is-it-it's-finally-happening*" thoughts making her want to scream with joy and cry at the same time. A lifetime of devotion, training and singular focus was culminating with this launch. She looked over at her fellow crew; their steely-eyed gazes roving the sea of switches, knobs, buttons and lights filled her with confidence. They were good men. No, *great* men.

And then, over the comm loops she heard Ray's throaty rasp confirming some expected weather activity in the mid-atmosphere.

There's another great man. If only...

She had to abort her train of thought as The Voice demanded her utmost concentration.

"...*three, two, one...ignition. Have a pleasant spaceflight!*"

Caitlin felt the familiar rumble as the vibrations of the Boeing consumed her. There were scarcely words to describe the incredible, unnatural amount of power coming to life beneath their feet. She cleared her mind of all things extraneous. As always, she would be mentally prepared for anything.

Outside, Caitlin could picture the support apparatus that held the great machine in place on the launch pad falling away. She felt the rocket lift from the ground. Then a rush took hold, a sense of duty combined with a familiar set of tasks she was capable of completing almost by rote, and she gave her mind over completely to the job of being an astronaut.

Two minutes later, passing through a cloud layer, she glanced back at the passengers and noticed a thin line of blood on the selenologist's forehead. Immediately, Caitlin heard the woman cry out through her headset. Caitlin was about to say something when a flash of bright light made her head turn.

The master alarm rang in her ears and her warning panel lit up like the tree at Rockefeller Center.

7 | MURPHY'S LAW

"Flight, this is Capsule Command, you read?" Caitlin repeated the question for the third time while Paul and Dallas tried to interpret the chaos of flashing instrument lights and braying alarms.

"Electrical system took a hit," Paul stated without emotion, throwing switches on the console with practiced skill.

"Ground comm's out," Caitlin said.

"We're still in the clouds," Dallas confirmed, eschewing instrumentation to look out the capsule window. "Three minutes, ten seconds post-launch. Losing gravity soon." Caitlin glanced down at the passengers again. Still strapped into their seats, still conscious. They were the priority. Asami Imura, the moon scientist, held two fingers of her right hand up to her forehead, but otherwise seemed alright. Caitlin was about to try the internal comm system to ask about the selenologist when a raspy voice crackled its way through her headset.

"...-opy that... —ing up, over."

Ray. Right now, his throaty rasp was the most beautiful voice in the world. "Ray, I copy. Lost you for a bit. Electrical's wonky, over."

"You took a lightning strike 180 seconds after liftoff," Ray said urgently. "We saw it—the bolt traveled all the way to the ground through your ionized gas plume. We lost flight telemetry for a few seconds but now it seems to be back."

The crew's eyes locked on one another with realization. "We saw a bright flash," Caitlin confirmed to Ray.

"Do me a favor and try switching Main to Aux," Ray said.

Paul found the switch and threw it. Instantly the Scrabble board of colored lights returned to normal.

"That did the trick," Caitlin relayed to Ray. She breathed a sigh of relief. They would not have to abort the mission.

Ray's next transmission confirmed that thought. "Proceed to parking orbit. We'll do diagnostics from there."

"Parking orbit" referred to a low-earth orbit trajectory where the spaceship could essentially sit idle and revolve safely around the Earth while the craft was examined.

"Copy that, Ray, we're punching through to LEO now. See you on the other side, over."

Ray's voice was replaced by another Controller's, and for the next several minutes a stream of technical chatter concerned with things like "escape velocity," "main engine burn," and "flight profile" filled the comm loops. Caitlin followed the conversation as she examined her controls, looking for signs that anything was not right. They only needed the big rocket for one more burn on the way to the moon—the one that would free them from Earth's orbit.

Something caught Caitlin's attention outside the window. Nothing specific, but a difference from moments before...*black sky*. She noted the dark velvet world outside her window, then looked back down at her controls.

Wait a minute. She whipped her head up and peered out the window again. With all the simulators she'd been in that provided realistic computer renderings to recreate specific flights, it had taken her a second to realize that this black sky was the real deal.

You're in space.

And then it grew eerily quiet as the roar and rumble of the main rocket engines cut out. Caitlin recognized the softer hiss of smaller thrusters that now leveled out their ship so that they wouldn't be tumbling end over end while orbiting the Earth.

Paul spoke into his comm unit. "Flight, Cap-Com here. Commencing diagnostics, over." A series of computer programs began checking for errors relating to the capsule's electrical system. Paul and Dallas monitored their progress while Caitlin turned and looked down into the crew bay.

All five passengers were still strapped to their seats, but she was surprised to see a tangible reminder that they had arrived in space.

A video camera floated in the weightlessness, seemingly suspended in midair as if by magic.

Blake pointed to the camera. "Really, I don't get off saying I told you so, Suzette."

The others turned their heads to follow Blake's finger. Their eyes lingered on the ultra high definition camcorder as it tumbled end-over-end in slow motion.

"God *damn* it, Suzette!" Asami Imura turned to glare at the Marketing VP. "Blake told you that thing was too big for the mount and you tried to force it anyway."

"Relax. It'll still work. Nobody got hurt."

Asami pulled her hand down from her forehead and turned her head in Suzette's direction. A thin gash across her right temple oozed blood. "What else are you going to be wrong about on this mission?"

James Burton had perked up considerably, shaking off the rush of the launch like a rider stepping off a rollercoaster and ambling away, wondering what else the park had in store. He scribbled in his pad, eyes darting from Asami's forehead to the suspended camera to its failed mounting bracket and back to his notes.

Blake's eyes widened at a developing situation he saw as a potential threat to Outer Limits' perfect safety record. The *Perfect Safety Record* must not be jeopardized. The space tourism industry was still in its infancy, and nothing but perfection would lead to further flights. If Outer Limits couldn't deliver, then there were half a dozen other private space outfits waiting in the wings—Black Sky chief among them. And they currently waited not in the wings, but on the moon, Blake reflected.

"Ladies, please. Relax. We followed protocol, the camera was secured, it came loose. No one is at fault."

"What about that flash of light—what was that?" This from Martin Hughes, who appeared a bit flushed from the experience, but contained.

"It happened right after I got hit by the camera," Asami said. "At first I thought I was seeing stars from being hit in the head. Scared the shit out of me," she finished, narrowing her eyes at Suzette.

"We were hit by lightning," Caitlin called down from the control deck. At this the passenger bay became silent. "No serious damage," Caitlin explained. "Flight Control just gave us the okay to head for the moon. We just wanted to double-check the capsule electrical system while in orbit before we made the rest of the trip."

Blake looked up at Caitlin and gave her a big smile and a thumbs-up sign. "The lightning is no one's fault, people, except maybe God's."

Martin, the exobiologist, winced at the statement. Then he swept a large hand out at the thick carpet of stars visible through one window and the blue Earth from the opposite. "You don't truly attribute all this to a god, do you, Blake? Surely He doesn't watch over us, at any rate, or we wouldn't have been struck by lightning in the first place, right?"

Blake let fly an exasperated sigh and was about to reply when a motion suddenly distracted him. The floating camera had slow-tumbled its way to within Asami's grasp. She snatched it out of the air, pressed the Record button and turned the cam around on herself.

"Next time, Suzette, you ask before you go changing specs on your own," she said, flipping the lens the bird. Then she flung it through the weightlessness back to Suzette, who never took her eyes off Asami as she cradled the spinning camera into her gut.

Asami stared the VP down but said nothing else as a drop of blood broke free from the gash on her temple. The scarlet globule floated before her eyes in the weightlessness, a crimson bauble representing a tiny but undeniable piece of her humanity.

"Medical," she calmly requested through her headset.

Dallas was there quickly. With expert, economical movements calculated to counteract the lack of gravity, he cleaned, sterilized and bandaged the skin over Asami's right eye.

"You're good to go," he pronounced, kicking off a bulkhead and grabbing strategically placed handholds to pull himself back "up" to the control deck, although that directional term no longer held any real meaning.

After a short countdown, the main engines fired and their craft accelerated deeper into space. Asami's suspended blood drop was thrust into motion, splashing into a window through which Caitlin could now see the moon.

8 | SEPARATION ANXIETY

Forty hours later

Caitlin Swain took a deep breath as she tried not to think about the quarter of a million miles that now separated her from home. The lunar surface slid beneath them from an altitude of about forty miles. During the last couple of days, she had watched the moon grow steadily larger in her window until now it filled her entire view. No longer simply a sphere hanging in blackness, the moon's surface was a grayscale world with visible terrain including vast craters, flat plains and epic mountain ranges. This lunar relief map was rife with navigational hazards for their fragile craft. Caitlin took two more deep breaths to calm her nerves while reminding herself that a small flotilla of robotic reconnaissance orbiters had, in the years prior to this mission, mapped out their landing region—and that of rival Black Sky—in ultra-high definition detail.

It both relaxed her and induced anxiety that she would have little control over their descent to the moon. Dallas Pace, M.D., their Lunar Module Pilot, was in charge of that crucial leg of their journey, and he was as competent as one could be who had never actually done it. Still, she thought, peering into a huge crater that occupied her entire field of view, and then spotting *another* crater deep inside of that one, she would be glad once they touched down safely.

Caitlin's current train of thought had begun about thirty minutes ago when they had transferred from the Command Module, where they'd cocooned for the last two days, to the Lunar Exploration Module. The LEM, as it was called for short, was actually larger than the Command Module since it would serve as their habitat while on the moon. At the end of their lunar stay, the LEM would take them back up to rendezvous with the Command Module for the return trip to Earth.

Caitlin and Dallas, instead of being seated above the passengers on a separate flight deck, were now situated on the same level as them but out to one side in a control alcove. Paul Abbott, as the Commander of the entire mission, would be the only member of the team to stay behind with the Command Module and orbit the moon while the other seven people rode the Lunar Module to the moon's surface.

Caitlin tore her eyes from the vivid moonscape outside her window. She glanced back at her passengers. They were seated in a circle around the perimeter of the LEM, mostly quiet since leaving the Command Module. Was it the realization that they were about to land on a planetary body other than Earth, Caitlin wondered, or was it just that they were all sick of each other already after two days in close confinement?

With the comm loops thick with pre-descent chatter buzzing in the background (Caitlin listened for Ray's voice but hadn't heard him since they went into lunar orbit), Martin Hughes wordlessly pointed out a mountain range to no one in particular. Asami Imura glanced around the circle, and when it seemed no one else had anything to say, offered, "Many people think of the moon as a flat boring place, maybe with some craters, but in reality it's home to mountains that are taller than our Mount Everest on Earth. Some of them are high enough, and at the right latitude such that they are never exposed to darkness. Peaks of Eternal Light."

Presently, Blake Garner dropped into the Lunar Module and took his seat in the circle, the last to do so. "Be nice to put some solar panels up there, eh?" he said, dropping into the conversation as well. "Endless energy!" Then, to Suzette, his videographer: "You filming? Did you get that? I want to remember that." She nodded.

Asami glared at her. "Why don't you stow that thing now so one of us doesn't get hurt?" In reply, Suzette swung the camera's lens her way.

"Doctor Imura, esteemed selenologist, how about if you tell us your thoughts as we orbit the moon, only minutes from descending on an alien world. Any insights so far?"

Asami was caught off guard by the serious question. She knew Suzette could edit out the line about getting hurt and just cut in with the question and awkward hesitation.

"Well," she began, "the moon—"

Suzette lowered her camera and put the lens cap on.

"—has had several geological forces acting on it, including volcanic activity, which…" Asami trailed off, stopping when she saw that Suzette was no longer filming. "Forget it," Suzette said, reaching behind her to put the camera into a storage compartment. "No one wants to hear it."

Asami's mouth dropped open in disbelief.

"I do. I'd like to hear it," Martin Hughes said.

The marketing veep shot him a withering stare. "We have a couple more minutes where I could have done it, but Safety Queen here's giving me a hard time. It was just for some B-roll stuff anyway, nobody wants to hear that crap."

Asami unclipped her seat harness. "I've had it with you." She started to stand up before the weightlessness made that difficult.

Dallas' voice came over the intercom. "We are go for Lunar Module separation in T-minus two minutes."

Blake held a hand out toward Asami in a stopping motion and shook his head. The selenologist resumed her seat. They were approaching the calculated point along their orbital path where their descent needed to begin if they were to end up at the target landing zone with minimal travel distance. "*Better* sit back down," Suzette said under her breath.

"*What*?" Asami leaned forward in her seat. "Blake, I didn't sign on to be abused by your crew."

Caitlin swiveled her command seat around to face the passengers. She'd read enough articles on the psychology of space travel to know that arguments such as these could be symptomatic of claustrophobia, agoraphobia, fear of the unknown and general stress. "Enough! After we land, you'll all get to stretch out a bit and eat. For now, we need you to sit back in your seats and relax."

Blake nodded his agreement, as did James Burton.

"Prepare for lander separation," Paul intoned.

"Let's light this candle," Dallas replied.

"Lunar Module, this is Command Module: You are go for descent burn."

They felt a rumbling surge, powerful but less so than the main rocket for Earth liftoff, and then the LEM departed from the rest of the spaceship.

"Have fun down there," Paul said. "I'll leave a light on for you."

9 | LANDING

Caitlin Swain sat close beside Dallas Pace in the lunar lander's control alcove as they powered toward the moon at a shallow angle. "Sat" wasn't really the right term though, because they descended with their backs toward the lunar surface, the current view out their window looking up and away from the moon into the black void of outer space. For most of the lander's descent, Dallas relied on an autopilot function preprogrammed with their landing site coordinates to keep them on course and to maintain a proper descent rate.

"Descent orbit insertion complete," Dallas announced, glancing at his instrumentation. "Descent engine cutoff in three...two...one..." The main descent engine was about to shut down, allowing the LEM to fall with lunar gravity until they were much closer to the lunar surface and the descent engine fired again, this time as a "brake." This procedure was necessary both to conserve fuel and to reduce their speed as they approached the lunar surface.

Caitlin raised her eyebrows when zero came and went but the roar of the main engine remained. She turned to look at Dallas who wore a puzzled expression. Caitlin had known him long enough to know he was a brilliant man—an astronaut as well as a medical doctor—and it wasn't often that he appeared puzzled by anything.

The comm loops exploded with chatter at the same time as a pair of red lights lit up on the console. Dallas was talking into his comm unit while pointing at a button on Caitlin's side of the console: Internal comm shutdown, *hit it, we need to talk in private.* Caitlin tapped it just before she heard someone say the words "program alarm."

She fought against a creeping fog of panic at the same time she saw Dallas' logic. It was the least she could do. All it did was cut the passengers out of the comm loops so they couldn't hear what was going on, but right now that was crucial. The last thing they needed was a panic onboard, and Blake would be furious to find out that Burton became privy to a Lunar Module Incident because she took her sweet time throwing the passenger comm kill switch.

Dallas took his transmitter offline and leaned in close to Caitlin without ceasing to manipulate the controls in front of him. "Something's wrong with the lunar landing guidance system."

Then, into his mic, he said, "Command Module, this is Lunar Module, commencing manual descent engine shutdown, over." Dallas' hands operated the controls with almost robotic precision, and in a few seconds Caitlin felt their craft decelerate as it became much quieter.

"Altitude 50,000 feet," Dallas said into his comm unit.

"That's way lower than we should be for descent engine cutoff," Caitlin said. They were still dropping down to the moon, now pulled by its gravity alone. They remained oriented upward, staring out into space.

Dallas touched Caitlin's arm, not a gesture of comfort or affection, but a signal he wanted her undivided attention. "Caitlin, listen. That lightning hit must have disabled the LEM's landing guidance. We only did diagnostics on the Command Module because the comm failure was a symptom there. I think maybe we should abort."

Caitlin took a deep breath as she considered this, staring into the pitch-blackness. They had the ability to jettison the descent engine and use the ascent engine—which ran off of a separate control program from the landing sequence—to hightail it back up to Paul in the orbiting Command Module. There would be no moon landing, but they'd all get back to Earth alive.

She slammed her fist onto the console in frustration. "For all we know there's something wrong with the ascent engine control program, too!" She knew Dallas didn't need her to spell out the implications for him. If the ascent stage engine burned too long, as the descent stage just had, they would miss the Command Module and go rocketing off into space without enough fuel to return to either lunar or Earth orbit. They'd die in the LEM when their oxygen ran out, drifting through the eternal vacuum of space in their metal coffin, possibly for years, until they burned up in some distant orbit.

Dallas bit his lip, a habit he had when in deep concentration. "It's either that or I land us manually."

Caitlin looked him in the eyes. He appeared as competent as ever. He wasn't panicking, his decision-making was solid. *Land us manually.* She exhaled deeply. His training had largely been on how to utilize the autopilot function to land, not to actually *fly* all the way down.

"For God's sake, Dallas," she whispered. She had no more words for the situation. Dallas understood it at least as well, and probably better, than she did.

"35,000 feet," Dallas said. They were now the same distance above the moon that commercial airliners flew above Earth.

Caitlin knew Dallas had been an Air Force test pilot before joining NASA, but still, that was two careers ago. She flashed on the lunar surface pockmarked with craters and scarred by mountains. Their selected landing site was a vast, flat plain—the same one Black Sky had already landed on—but they had veered off course.

Then Caitlin heard Ray's voice over the comm channels, urgently discussing something about a descent trajectory with another Controller. The impulse to return to Earth was unbearably strong. The urge to abort was powerful. But if there was one thing Caitlin feared above all else, it was suffocating in this cramped vehicle while she told Ray she loved him over a damn comm unit. *No way. I'd rather blow up on lunar impact.*

She spoke rapidly. "If we land, we'll be able to troubleshoot the ascent stage before we take off again."

Dallas nodded immediately, urging the conversation on while eyeing his gauges. "Right, exactly. If we land."

"Can you do it?"

"I think so."

"Then let's go for it."

"Switch on the landing radar, please, and call out our altitude at regular intervals."

Caitlin smiled as she carried out his command. Dallas was one cool cucumber. She heard the *hiss* of the attitude thrusters as the spacecraft rolled about its vertical axis, putting them in a normal sitting position with respect to the lunar surface.

"10,000 feet, we should be in braking phase!" Caitlin said. And then she looked out the window where she now looked down on the world of the moon.

"Mountain!"

"I have it on radar." A mountain top passed below them and to the north, a reminder that they could *crash* here, just like flying a small airplane on Earth, like the Cessna she owned back home.

For the next thirty minutes, Dallas carried out the precise order of operations with which the LEM's autopilot had been painstakingly programmed by a team of engineers. Adjusting the ship's altitude this way and that, initiating the braking sequence where the main descent engine had to be fired for just the right amount of time to counter the LEM's rate of descent, all the while monitoring their speed, position and systems status. Even the comm loops remained mostly quiet. There was nothing anybody else could do.

"1,000 feet," Caitlin said.

She peered into the dark depths of a crater, the ground dropping out beneath them until their little capsule whizzed over the crater's rim and emerged back over flat ground.

"500 feet!"

"Landing phase," Dallas announced. "Fuel?"

"One minute remaining!"

Dallas' hands raced across the controls as he engaged thrusters to adjust their position. They needed to land upright on the LEM's footpads. To reach the surface in any other position would be catastrophic.

"200 feet. Thirty seconds."

"And..." Dallas burned the last of the descent engine's fuel to slow their fall. Caitlin watched in horror as she saw the grayish soil rush up at her, swirls of lunar dust displaced by the engine's thrust.

"Contact!" Dallas said as they hit the ground.

Caitlin's head was pitched forward in a whiplash motion, but not all the way into the console in front of her. It reminded her of the time as a teenager when she plowed her Jetta into a car stopped at a light, at about twenty miles per hour. It was a hard landing, but blessedly short of a full-on crash.

Dallas shut down the engine and other flight systems.

"Lunar Module to Mission Control: we have touchdown."

The moon dust dissipated around their craft while excited cheers burst through the comm loops. They both had their first look out the window. They had landed on somewhat uneven ground, the LEM canted slightly to one side, but it was a lot better than coming down on the side of a crater or on top of a mountain, where they could roll all the way down.

Caitlin leaned over and gave Dallas a hug. "Thank you."

"Don't thank me just yet," Dallas said, looking at their lunar position display. "Let's see where we are first."

"I'll handle that, you take a break." Caitlin consulted the display and compared it to their stored landing point.

She frowned. "We're a mile away from our designated touchdown coordinates, and unfortunately that puts us closer than we should be to Black Sky's landing site." The rival space outfits had an agreement with one another—a formal, signed agreement—to share the large optimal landing site, but at a minimum distance away from each other at all times. This landing mishap put them much closer to Black Sky's territory than they should be according to that agreement. "Blake's not going to be happy," Caitlin summed up.

Dallas pursed his lips, concentrating. "Let's see, what could we say? Solar winds blew us off course?" They both laughed, blowing off some steam, until they felt a hand on each of their shoulders.

"Excellent job! A tad bumpy, but here we are! Are we free to move about the cabin?" Blake Garner grinned at the astronauts, not yet aware of what had transpired.

Dallas turned around. "You bet," he managed. He was too exhausted to attempt an explanation just yet.

Blake walked from the control alcove, once again under the influence of gravity, back to the passengers. He raised his arms in a sweeping motion toward the two windows on either side of the LEM.

"Ladies and gentlemen, welcome to the moon! Shall we step outside?"

10 | ONE SMALL STEP

Once James had donned his spacesuit and triple-checked the oxygen gauge, he stared hard at the door to the lunar module, suddenly overcome by trepidation. Maybe he'd simply watched too many science fiction movies as a teenager, but gazing out the window, the moon looked about as inviting as a swimming pool filled with razor blades under a rubbing-alcohol rain.

There's no air out there.

But then, there was no air when he and his wife Deana went scuba diving off the coast of Grand Cayman on the vacation they took to celebrate their 25th anniversary. Was this really all that much different than that?

Yes, James. Yes, it is. This isn't the azure Caribbean with white sand beaches under coconut palms a short swim away. It's the goddamn moon. A gray world where no life can exist at all.

At least that was the expert opinion of every known scientist on Earth. But Blake seemed to have been hinting otherwise. And why else would he have an exobiologist along, such an expensive seat to fill for someone not already on Blake's payroll? He supposed it could be simply to confirm that there is indeed no life on the moon.

The thought that no one really knew much about whatever was up here—out there— scared the hell out of him, too. The comm channels crackled to life with the voices of the other passengers as one by one, they got into their suits and spoke into their radios.

"Suzette," Blake said over the common channel. "I want you out   the   door   first."

"Really? I thought you'd prefer the honor."

"Nonsense. I need you to capture my first steps and words on video for posterity."

"Can't you do that while I stand on the steps of the lunar module?"

"No, I want the ship in the background."

Behind his helmet, Burton rolled his eyes. Martin, meanwhile, was paying the entire scene no mind, just staring up at the starry void.

Asami came up beside James with a smile that could melt glass. Burton wondered if Blake had told her to flirt with him a little, to butter him up? He wouldn't put it past him. At the same time, he wasn't above needing a little inspiration. Had it not been for the two helmets, he'd have been inclined to ask for a good luck kiss. *Well, probably not, but what does it really matter now?*

"Careful out there, Mr. Burton. But don't forget to have fun!" She gave his shoulder a pat and stepped aside to give him plenty of room to make his exit.

He thanked her, although "be careful" was just about the last thing he wanted to hear. He'd have been much happier with, "Go on, you big wuss. There's nothing whatsoever to worry about. It's as safe as an English garden out there."

The hiss of the hatch opening reminded James of his wife's cat, Grey Skies, back on Earth. A fine temperament for a feline, but he made that startling sound any time James accidently stepped on his fluffy gray tail during one of his middle-of-the-night jaunts to the kitchen.

James walked slowly to the edge and looked out onto the moon. *The moon!* Blake was down there already, standing about ten feet away from the LEM, carefully positioning himself for Suzette's camera. About ten more feet behind him, Suzette aimed her video device toward Blake and the ship. In the LEM, Martin and Asami waited patiently for James to get some balls and leave the capsule.

He looked back out onto the moon once and stared down the ladder, thinking of Neil Armstrong's first descent. He instantly felt the hair on his forearms stand on end. *One rung at a time*, he told himself.

He dangled a foot over the side and took a leap of faith. His momentum carried his next foot over, and he suddenly feared tumbling like an idiot down the stairs, perhaps cracking his helmet open in the process. Wouldn't that be ironic, he couldn't help but think, visualizing a sensational news headline. *FAA Safety Administrator Killed on Moon Due to Own Carelessness.* Wonderful. People would love that, too. He reminded himself why he was here. Just go through the experience and report back. He'd heard there was already a 68-year-old woman signed up to ride on the second flight once Outer Limits got clearance. If she could do it...

He slowed, steadied himself. Allowed himself a look at the terrain just ahead of him, and reflected on the description Armstrong had relayed back to the scientists on Earth.

"The surface appears to be very, very fine grained as you get close to it; it's almost like a powder..." Too many adverbs, of course. Rather than an astronaut, Burton thought, they should have sent a man of letters to the moon in 1969.

Another foot forward and James dropped onto the surface of Earth's only natural satellite. Again, he heard Armstrong's voice instead of his own.

"That's one small step for man...one giant leap for mankind." Poor guy, that Armstrong. Responsible for uttering some of the most important words in human history and he got them wrong. He'd meant to say, "That's one small step for *a* man...one giant leap for mankind." The way Armstrong said it made no sense at all. *One small step for Man. One giant leap for mankind.* Man and mankind were one and the same without that article. That single, solitary letter – that *a* – had been absent for generations and would remain absent for generations to come.

The next few steps James took came easy, almost *too* easy. He must have appeared to the others as though he were skipping. He was practically weightless here on the moon, yet maintained every scintilla of his strength.

Cautiously, he turned, admiring the deep footprints he'd left on the moon's surface.

Then he looked up to see Blake Garner waving at him.

"Congratulations!"

"Thanks."

Suzette played with the camera for a moment before pointing it in the direction of the LEM. "Ready to shoot."

Raising his arms in a display of victory, Blake cleared his throat and spoke loudly through his headset.

"We stand today on the edge of a new frontier," he began.

They waited for more but there was no more to come. Blake simply bounded off away from the LEM with an exaggerated fist pump.

"That's it?" James said to Suzette, momentarily forgetting Blake could hear. "Isn't that JFK speaking of the 1960s?"As best she could in her spacesuit, Suzette shrugged.

"He worked on that for days. Every other phrase he threw at me came from *Star Trek.*"

Blake boldly turned around about ten feet from the ship. "If you have something better, Suzette, write it down and attribute it to me. Otherwise, keep the color commentary inside your own helmet, please."

"Of course," she said as Asami Imura started down the steps.

James' instinct was to rush forward in order to greet her at the bottom, to help her avoid the tumble he'd nearly taken himself, or at least imagined he had. But then he reminded himself that he was here to gauge the safety of the entire experience for future space tourists. It wasn't his place to physically help people anymore than it was a lifeguard's job to make sure the pool's construction techniques were up to code. No, Burton's job was to observe how things went and then to point out how it could be safer, highlighting any potential dangers he had noticed. Asami was far more graceful than he had been getting down the ladder, though, and before he knew it she was standing there next to him on the moon, definitely not in need of his help.

"It's beautiful," she said, as they took in the moonscape, that endless desert of gray. Personally, he thought it was boring as shit. A lot of gray rock, pretty flat but with some hills in the distance.

Well, she is a selenologist after all; this giant rock is *her life's work.* James swung back around to face her. "The moon is all it was cracked up to be, I presume?"

"Not the moon," Asami said, staring intently over his shoulder.

"Then what?" James turned to follow her gaze. "The stars?"

Her gloved hand tightened around his as he stole a glance at the sky and the wondrous blue-green sphere, sitting like an angel on

Luna's shoulder. Asami exhaled deeply, a sound so soft it felt as though her lips were pressed right against his ear. Then she whispered into her headset a single word that made him shiver. Made him question again why in the Hell he had come all the way up here when he had so much to live for down there. Already his mind was getting a little weird, wondering what his wife would think of him holding hands with this woman nearly half his age through a spacesuit.

"Earth."

Then Martin Hughes stepped down from the LEM and Blake Garner stood in front of their small group and tested his headset again. Once he was certain every one of them could hear, he launched into a well-rehearsed monologue, addressing each of the group by name before speaking while Suzette rolled the camera.

"Welcome to Luna. Eight years ago, Outer Limits began carrying private passengers to an altitude of sixty-two miles, just outside of Earth's atmosphere, into the blackness of space. For a quarter of a million dollars, ticket holders were able to experience three full days of pre-flight preparation, including how to make the most of their time in microgravity, before setting off on what would surely be the journey of their lives. Saudi sheiks, South American heads of state, Japanese businessmen, international celebrities, and American socialites all witnessed the awe of being a true astronaut, of traveling at speeds of nearly twenty-five hundred miles per hour – three times the speed of sound – before being released from their restraints in order to enjoy a zero gravity environment. But of course, that was just the beginning for the rapidly growing industry of space tourism."

Blake swiveled his head from left to right, searching the lunar grounds, no doubt still amazed himself by the desolation of the moonscape.

"Today," he continued, "Outer Limits has taken you – a privileged few – to a new world. The *New* New World, if you will. With the successful conclusion of this flight, the moon is now officially a tourist destination for almost any individual on Earth with the means to fulfill their dreams." As James listened, he tried his best to read Blake's face behind the helmet. The magnate seemed preoccupied, perhaps even dismayed by something.

Yet as he rambled on about the magnificence of the moon, about Outer Limits' unrivaled focus on safety, his own grandiose plans for stations and bases, housing and eventually amusement parks, his confidence seemed to swell back to normal levels.

Well, normal at least for Blake Garner. Overinflated for anyone else.

"Someday in the near future, the moon will represent more than simply a premiere space experience package. A few men and women and children – this century's *pioneers* – will call Earth's natural satellite their *home*. Not their home away from home, mind you, but *home*."

As James looked around the dry, dusty gray world, he found it difficult to believe anyone would ever want to call this place home, fancy habitat or not. Then again, he never imagined he'd even be standing up here, either, so who knew? By now he felt comfortable enough to move to within a few feet behind Suzette, who had her camera focused on Blake's helmet. He tried to be surreptitious but swiftly learned that was a losing battle here on the moon. His movements were far too clumsy and exaggerated to manage any kind of stealth. He squinted in order to get a better image of Blake's facial expressions. Was he calm, in control, or faking it? But what he really wanted was not only to get into Blake's helmet, but to get into his head. Because...and he wasn't sure how he knew—call it a flight safety inspector's sixth sense—he still sensed something was wrong, very wrong. And only Blake seemed to know what that was.

Blake took a step back. "As I am sure our moon scientist, the esteemed Dr. Asami Imura, can attest to you in far greater detail, the world on which we are now standing was most likely formed some four-point-five billion years ago, when the newly formed proto-Earth was struck by another celestial body the size of Mars. That magnificent impact blasted vast amounts of material into orbit around the Earth..."

Blake trailed off for a moment, turning his head to the left as though he'd heard someone calling out from behind him. When he continued, his voice wavered a bit, as though filled with uncertainty and trepidation.

"...which eventually coalesced to form the moon."

"Is something wrong, Blake?" Martin Hughes stepped closer to the business mogul.

Blake turned to glare again. "Not wrong," he said at a near whisper. "Just off."

Burton kept his own face expressionless behind his helmet. He'd mastered his poker face over the decades after learning early on that people would ask *What's the matter?* if they saw him make any kind of facial gesture while on an inspection. He didn't want them picking up on certain things he was noticing either, or they might be corrected before he submitted his report, and contested later. He could tell by looking at the helmets of the others that if there was any kind of reflection you couldn't see behind the faceplate, but he was taking no chances. Plus, he had to admit, resuming his old work habits had a calming effect on him, even up here on the moon. With six weeks to retirement, he wasn't about to start breaking old routines now.

Blake turned to face away from the others. "Garner to Pace. Come in, Pace."

A moment later, Dallas' voice was in James' ear. "Pace here. Go ahead, sir."

"Switch frequencies, Pace."

"Switching frequencies."

Their voices cut out of the common loop.

James watched as Blake's finger pointed in the direction of a nearby crater. According to what he'd read, there were more than 300,000 craters wider than one kilometer on the moon's near side alone. The great majority of these craters —now named for explorers, scientists, scholars, and artists — were said to be formed by asteroids and comets colliding with the lunar surface.

James stared up at the Earth, which he found after a few seconds to have a dizzying effect on him. Everything he'd ever known was way over there on that little blue marble... He forced himself to look away and then checked his oxygen levels again. They appeared fine, yet his head felt fuzzy, as though he'd just woken from a twisting-and-turning sleep. Perhaps it was from peering up into black space rather than a true blue sky. He lowered his head in an attempt to recover. He stepped back over to Asami and she squeezed his hand again. She bent forward to make eye contact through the helmets. She mouthed the words, "You okay?" He was grateful for her silent communication, not wanting the entire group to think he couldn't hack it already. He nodded in return and released his grip from hers, pressed his gloved hands against his thighs when the wooziness failed to abate. James' eyes fixated on the lunar surface, on the ubiquitous gray dust that seemed so unfitting for such a magnificent world.

Like a fiddler crab stirring just below the sand, the gray dust at his feet shifted ever so slightly.

Then abruptly stopped.

Had it even moved at all?

Of course not. There was no breeze on the moon. No atmosphere at all. That fact had caused more than a few feeble-minded conspiracy theorists to claim that no man had ever actually walked on the moon, that the entire Apollo 11 mission was a fake conjured to humiliate the Russians by winning the so-called Space Race. There is a famous photograph of Neil Armstrong and Buzz Aldrin planting the American flag on the lunar surface. In the picture, the flag appears to be waving in the wind. Of course, there's a simple explanation for this. The 3' x 5' nylon flag had been altered by sewing a hem along the top and inserting a crossbar hinged to the flagpole. Had these measures not been taken, the flag would have appeared limp and lifeless, not at all befitting the momentous event.

As his heart rate slowed, James stared at the surface for several more minutes, but nothing moved. He'd been seeing things. Now that the dizziness had faded, his eyes were finally adjusting and the dust appeared still once again.

He promised himself he'd speak to Dallas about his symptoms as soon as he could.

11 | EXTRAVEHICULAR ACTIVITY

Caitlin Swain was all too glad to leave the LEM's control alcove, where Dallas Pace was breaking the news to their boss that they had landed significantly off course. As she stepped into the airlock, she could hear Dallas explaining patiently to Blake Garner, "Absolutely not, sir, we cannot move the lander except for when we take off to meet Paul up in orbit. There is not enough fuel to do so."

Caitlin shook her head as she pressurized the airlock, which was the size of a walk-in closet with two sealed doors, one leading into the LEM and one to the outside. *Move the lander just because the area's a little different and he won't be able to give the exact tour he rehearsed for days on end, sure! That's space travel for you! Deal with it.* But as she donned her spacesuit, she grew somber. She was part of the technical expertise Blake had hired, and as such it was her job to help him make this mission a success. *It's precisely because of the fact that Blake doesn't know what he's doing that you're here. So don't make fun of him, help him. That's your job.*

She snapped her helmet into place and activated the comm system to the frequency Dallas and Blake were using. "...too close to Black Sky's landing site, damn it! You have to move!"

"Once again, sir, as it is I'm going to need to run thorough diagnostics ship-wide, especially on the ascent stage, to make sure we don't have another guidance control issue resulting from that lightning hit. That would need to be completed before we can even think about moving the LEM. We're stuck where we are, sir. We'll just have to make the best of it."

Dallas was so calm and in control, Caitlin thought. She wished she could be more like him. She wanted to yell at Blake, *You're lucky we didn't abort the landing altogether! You should be glad we're here at all, in one piece!* Blake uttered a few choice oaths and then told Dallas to keep him updated.

"Copy that, sir. I'll keep you posted. Have fun out there and stay safe."

Caitlin cut in. "Swain here, boys. I'm go for EVA, over."

"Copy that, Caitlin , you are go for EVA," Dallas returned.

"Hurry up if you can." This from Blake. " We're behind schedule because of this unfamiliar terrain. And switch back to the common frequency now, but make no mention of the landing screw-up."

She bit back an acidic reply, something about how the "screw-up" had given him the chance to complete his mission when most astronauts would have either aborted or crashed. *Be like Dallas.*

"On my way, sir." She hit a button and the outer airlock door slid up. She sucked her breath in sharply as she took in the mind-blowing moonscape with the Earth suspended above in a tapestry of black. It was much different than even looking through the LEM's windows. At last she was witness to the "magnificent desolation" Buzz Aldrin had spoken of decades earlier. She waved to the group assembled nearby in a loose circle. Blake returned the gesture first, his wave appearing stiff and exaggerated in the space suit.

A couple of the others were facing away from the LEM. In addition to the Outer Limits logo prominently displayed on the front of the suits, there were large name patches sewn onto both the front and back of their custom-fitted spacesuits. HUGHES appeared to be gazing at the Earth in a trance, while GARNER seemed to be preoccupied with the lunar dirt, along with IMURA. BURTON was watching Caitlin intently. The rest were facing Blake, including CALDERON, who was filming.

The astronaut backed carefully down the ladder and dropped onto the lunar surface with a puff of dust.

"Well hello, Caitlin!" Blake said. "Glad you could join us. Ladies and gentlemen, I believe our Command Module Pilot has a surprise for us. Something not on the itinerary."

"You bet!" Caitlin took a few steps to the right, walking along the outside of the LEM. She stopped in front of a rectangular flat panel and flipped a switch. "I'm guessing you didn't know that we had a garage on the lunar lander." The panel slid to one side to reveal what looked like a storage area of some kind behind it. Inside it was dark, but when Suzette turned the video camera on it, its light revealed wheels, a chassis, and a parabolic dish.

"Walking long distances on the moon is dangerous and consumes more of our precious oxygen," Caitlin said, squeezing into the garage alongside the object it contained. "And so, like some of the legendary Apollo missions before us, we've brought our own surface transportation."

Blake nodded his hearty approval, the image of the group gathered around him bobbing crazily up and down in his helmet's faceplate as Caitlin climbed into the seat of the vehicle. When she looked out on the group, she was pleased to see Suzette pointing the camera her way.

Caitlin pressed a button to activate the vehicle's electrical system. She turned on the headlights—totally unnecessary and a waste of battery power, but Blake had told her to do it anyway because it would "look fantastic on the video." She pressed her foot to the accelerator, hearing the faint hum common to electric vehicles, and rolled out of the garage toward the group.

"Behold our very own lunar rover," Blake said, "or, as I like to call it—the moon buggy!" Outer Limits had clearly been inspired by the original Apollo design—wire wheels, a lightweight frame of aluminum alloy tubing, seats of canvas webbing, and a dish antenna. But there were differences, too. It carried four seats instead of two. And the battery, while weighing less, was a significantly more powerful lithium design. Video cameras were mounted front and rear and a GPS unit sat next to the vehicle's hand controls.

But Caitlin knew that Blake's favorite thing about the rover was that Black Sky didn't have one. An Outer Limits exclusive you'll only get when you join the premiere space experience tour.

"But don't worry," Blake said as he walked past Caitlin in the rover and to the LEM, where he opened a second panel adjacent to the first to reveal another garage. "I know what you're thinking. There are six of us out here but only four seats." He stepped in and inside of a minute had parked a second rover beside Caitlin 's.

"That's why we brought two," he said, beaming. *Outer Limits: 2, Black Sky: 0.*

Five minutes later, the two rovers drove away from the LEM toward the crater that they had flown over during their landing escapade. James Burton rode shotgun next to Caitlin, while the selenologist had the back seat. In the other vehicle, Blake drove while Martin Hughes sat beside him, and Suzette occupied both back seats for herself and her camera equipment.

The comm channels buzzed with excitement as the moon buggies bounced and jostled over the uneven landscape. James pestered Caitlin with technical questions about the range, speed and handling capabilities of the rovers while behind her, Asami and Martin discussed which was more beautiful, the moon or the Earth, or was it really both of them in concert that imparted the other with its true beauty? Blake was quieter, eyes focusing often on the vehicle controls, especially the GPS, with Suzette taking footage from the back of his rover as they bounded along the lunar surface.

The rovers came to a small hillock and Blake stopped atop its crest. Caitlin followed suit and pulled up next to him so that she was now across from Dr. Hughes. In front of them, the hillock leveled out into a flat plain, one that soon rose sharply to meet the crater wall. The crater's exterior was a formidable hill with a gradual but long incline that Caitlin judged to be several stories high at the rim. She looked past Martin at Blake, who was fussing with the GPS unit and talking. Except that she couldn't hear what he was saying, which meant that he'd switched over to the other frequency to speak with Dallas. He was lost, asking for directions to where his planned site was from here. She watched as he threw up his hands and swiveled his head around. Then she heard his voice.

"Let's take a drive to the rim of the crater. Make sure to stop short of the actual top—we don't need anyone falling in. The view will be marvelous."

Blake led the way up in a zigzag pattern, as if driving up switchbacks that had yet to be carved into the hill's face. Stealing a glance behind them, Caitlin reflected that their tire tracks were indeed the modest beginnings of a new road. With no wind to blow them away, they were a permanent environmental modification. A half an hour later, both rovers rested about twenty feet from the rim. Blake was right about one thing, Caitlin thought, gazing back down from where they'd come. The view was spectacular. She could see their lunar lander, a squat metal object, at once so tiny and so fragile and so utterly foreign on this stark world of rock and dust.

"Our home away from home," Blake said, pointing out the LEM while Suzette followed his finger with the camera. "Let's have a look, shall we?" Blake exited the rover and bunny-hopped the rest of the way to the uppermost portion of the rim. More cautiously, the others, including Caitlin, followed suit.

Standing on the lip of the crater, Caitlin was speechless with awe when confronted with the sheer size of the crater's interior. It had to be a mile wide. As if in response to her thoughts, Asami said, "It looks impressive, but this is a relatively small crater."

"It's too steep here," Blake said, turning on his heel and bounding back down to his rover.

"Too steep for what?" James Burton asked.

"C'mon, we need to go 'round a bit more."

They all piled back into the vehicles, and after another half an hour, just as the first stirrings of "Hey, maybe we should head back," were on peoples' lips, Blake stopped his rover near the rim again, consulted his GPS with a frown, and got out.

Caitlin followed him to the rim, a few feet away. The interior of the crater was not as steep here. In fact, it would be possible to walk down into it were one so inclined. But as Blake began to encourage the others to have a look into the crater, a glint down on the ground and far in the distance was flagged by Caitlin's peripheral vision.

"Those are some interesting geological features," Asami was saying as she peered into the crater. "You see that?" But Caitlin no longer heard her. She was squinting onto the lunar plain at the base of the crater, looking at a lunar lander. But their LEM was miles back in the other direction. There was no way they should be able to see it from here, as it should be blocked by the mountainous crater. Had they already gone all the way around it?

Impossible.

She was about to raise the question with Blake but by the time she turned around and composed her thoughts, the group was already following her boss down into the crater.

"It's just a short nature walk from here," he called out, already out of view.

Taking one more look back at the strange LEM, it hit her: they had landed so far off course that they had strayed into the territory of their rivals, to the very part of the moon they had signed a treaty of sorts saying they wouldn't venture to.

Black Sky was here.

12 | MOONWALKING

"I have to tell you, Blake, I don't think this is wise from a commercial standpoint," James Burton's voice said somewhere up ahead of Caitlin. More like *down ahead*, she thought, looking up at the crater's lip from the outside face. The rest of the team had already topped over the rim and were now making their way down the inside of the crater. But there was no way she felt comfortable leaving these rovers parked on the crater incline without wheel chocks to keep them from rolling. She found the chocks and placed them underneath the moon buggies' wheels to make certain the rovers couldn't roll down the outside of the crater while they were away. Her rover training back home had been kept secret so as not to tip off Blake's "surprise excursion feature," as he called it—he was paranoid that Black Sky would get wind of it and do the same thing.

Climbing the steep outer face of the crater was tricky going in the light gravity, and Caitlin relegated the group conversation to the back of her mind while she concentrated on her footing.

"Because, Blake," Burton was transmitting to the team, "to do this moon walk you're relying on multiple systems with insufficient redundancy. Do we have enough air in our suits to walk back to the lander if something happened to one of the rovers, or if we got lost and couldn't find them again?"

"We landed a bit further away than I aimed to, James, I admit that, but I think the fact that we are still able to do this crater walk demonstrates our flexibility and how agile our overall setup really is."

"But this is a more professional team than you plan to take up here, when any old billionaire will be able to afford a ticket. These are scientists and Outer Limits personnel and astronauts we've got with us. What's it going to be like when you have some guy and his wife up here just because they happen to own a professional sports team or they bought some stock at the right time?"

"Speaking of astronauts," Blake said, "Caitlin —where are you?"

"Just a few steps from the rim. Had to set the wheel chocks, over."

"Caitlin, I want you down here with us, now! We don't split up."

"Copy that, Blake, I just needed to—"

"Now, Command Module Pilot Swain! Am I understood?"

"Copy that, sir." Caitlin shook her head and took one last look at the rover before she started back up the crater. *It'll hold. Time to play Astronaut Tour Guide.* It irked her that Blake would put her extensive and demanding training to use as little more than a glorified chaperone, but then again, she thought, reaching the lip of the crater again, he had given her the moon, which was something no one else had been able to do, even NASA.

Blake's voice droned on in her helmet as she steadied herself. "As I was saying, James, we're perfectly capable of modifying the tour to suit our clientele. I realize you're used to the rather rigid operating guidelines of a government bureaucracy, but we're a small, agile company, able to...."

Resting on the lip of the crater before making the descent into the interior after the rest of the team, Caitlin saw the undulating hills of the moon below, with the mysterious Black Sky lander off in the distance to her right. *Now is not the time to ask about that,* she thought. Raising her line of sight, she saw the moon's horizon—much closer than that of Earth.

The moon was only a quarter the size of the blue planet, and she could see the curvature of it. Even without being on top of a crater, the close horizon made her feel as though she stood atop a giant hill, rather than on a real planetary body. The effect was disorienting and a little unnerving. Up here on top of a crater, it was even more so. She forced herself to look away from the horizon before the onset of vertigo could take hold. Her eyes focused on the Earth beyond. She thought of Ray, spinning around on that blue-and-white sphere, talking to Paul and Dallas on the comm loops, making sure their mission was under control. And it hit her at that moment, with a team of moon walkers waiting for her inside a lunar crater. For all of her astronaut aspirations and lifelong dreams of other worlds, nothing could ever be more precious to her than home. She did not want to die here on this barren rock in the void of space.

As she had discussed over drinks at FlyBoyz with fellow space junkies at their happy hour spot near the spaceport, at any given time while on the lunar surface you were a maximum of two system failures away from death.

Taking a deep breath, Caitlin scrubbed these thoughts from her mind with an equally deep exhalation. Then she stepped off the rim down into the crater. The group was maybe fifty yards down the face, approaching a rock outcropping, the bottom of the crater far, far below that. The suit names were unreadable at this distance, but she saw one of the figures raise his or her arms in some kind of exclamatory gesture.

Martin Hughes asked, "Is there ice down here in this crater?"

"There's no ice down here," Asami declared flatly, using a pair of tongs to pluck a lunar rock from the ground. She placed it into a plastic bag. Caitlin knew that part of Asami's responsibilities consisted of overseeing a "sample return" objective where moon rocks would be brought back home. Having an outside selenologist declare the sampling techniques to be scientifically sound would prevent skeptics from claiming that their samples had been contaminated because they didn't adhere to accepted collection techniques. Never mind that most of the moon rocks would end up in the hands of CEOs who were in a position to return the favor someday to Blake Garner, exotic paperweights that would inevitably end up on eBay when a big enough financial meteor storm made an appearance.

"Sunlight reaches all the way to the bottom," Asami continued while zipping the specimen bag shut. "The only lunar ice we know about so far is found in the polar craters."

"Oh c'mon, Dr. Buzzkill," Martin said, "there *could* be a pocket of ice down here somewhere under some rock heap."

"No, she's right," Blake cut in. "There's no ice down here."

Caitlin hopped her way down the slope, finding it much easier going compared to the outside of the crater.

Below her, Martin halted his forward progress and stood there motionless.

James Burton took advantage of the silence. "Blake, don't think I overlooked the fact that you haven't addressed my concerns." He was a few feet behind Blake, who made his way around the side of the rock formation that they could now see was almost twenty feet high.

"I believe I have partially addressed them." Blake disappeared around the outcropping. "But allow me to add that no one has to stay with us down here if they don't want to. I can have Caitlin take anyone who wants to back to the rovers to await our return. Just say the word. That will go for our tourist EVAs as well."

"Some people might feel too embarrassed to speak up like that in a group setting, over open communications channels," Burton pointed out. "They'll be forced to go along with the group against their better judgment."

Blake gave an exaggerated sigh from around the other side of the rocks. "Follow me this way, people. We're almost there."

13 | DESCENT

Caitlin heard the rasping hiss of Blake's breath as he apparently made a move requiring exertion, before continuing. "James, they can switch over to a private channel to express their wishes if they want. I'm sure we can devise some kind of alert system, but really—they came here to explore! These early lunar tourists aren't your typical family who goes to the Grand Canyon on vacation, who want to drive to the lookout, take a couple of pictures and go, 'Okay, we saw that! Let's go get some fast food!' No, the clients we cater to will, in all likelihood, be more like the adventurous souls who hike down into the Canyon and then go whitewater rafting at the bottom, camping out for a few days before trekking back out."

"Well that's funny, Mr. Garner, because your brochure states quite prominently, 'Our lunar landing trips are designed to be enjoyed by any able-bodied person. If you can endure a transoceanic flight on a commercial airplane and then walk across the terminal to make your connection, then you are able to participate in our premiere space experience product.' Or some such drivel."

"Hey, I wrote that!" Suzette turned around to face Burton as he made his way around the outcropping. James did not apologize.

Caitlin scanned the crater further down towards the floor, and she noted that there were several such outcroppings dotting the landscape. The one they had reached just happened to be the highest up.

Suzette raised her camera to her shoulder to aim it in Blake's direction. "And there's an asterisk that refers to the fine print where it says they have to pass the physical first."

"I'm rolling my eyes inside my helmet right now," Burton responded. "Because I suspect a diabetic Alzheimer's patient could pass your physical if they had the financial wherewithal to—"

"Right here, people!" Blake exclaimed, cutting James off. "This is what I want you to see. Gather around, come on."

A couple of minutes later, all six of them stood huddled around Blake on the other side of the outcropping. Blake stood proudly, feet planted firmly apart, head held high, pointing into a chasm of some kind.

"Is that a cave?" Asami asked.

"It is," Blake said, "although it's more like a tunnel system than a cavern. There's an extensive network of passages underneath our feet."

"Extraordinary," Asami said. "I'll have to check for anomalies in the strata signatures on our satellite maps when I get back. It's possible that—"

Blake cut her off with a wave of the hand. "I do apologize, Dr. Imura, but we have a schedule to keep here. We're following a very carefully planned itinerary," he finished, deliberately turning to face James Burton, who said nothing as he stared transfixed into the geological aperture.

"Flip on your helmet lights, please," Blake said, a beam originating from atop his helmet slicing into the blackness of the tunnel. They could see a tight rocky throat that wound quickly out of sight down and to the left. One by one, piercing rays of light emanated from xenon bulbs as the group activated their helmet lamps.

Caitlin watched as Blake's lips moved without her being able to hear. *He's telling Dallas we're about to go underground.*

The entire group stood facing the tunnel except for James, who was kicking at the soil for some reason with his right foot.

Blake looked at the group. "Are we ready?"

"Hold on," Suzette said. She was typing into a handheld electronic device, one with an input interface large enough to accommodate her spacesuit gloves. "I need to update the Outer Limits social network feeds..." A series of grunts and under-breath remarks made it clear the group was not happy about this. Even

Blake tilted his head to one side while staring at her, a gesture of impatience.

Suzette   spoke   as   she   typed. "On…super…cool…moonwalk…now…over&out!" She packed the device away and replaced it with her running video camera. "Ready!" she proclaimed.

"Let's go, people." Blake led the way into the tunnel, ducking his head as he stepped inside. A few feet in, he stopped. Turned.

"Suzette, shut the camera off."

14 | MISSION CONTROL

Back in Las Cruces, New Mexico, Flight Controller Ray McCullough wiped the guacamole from his chin as he reentered the control room. The scruff on his face left several long white lines across the deeply tanned skin of his forearm.

"Missed a little," fellow Flight Controller Jerry Ableton said as Ray passed his station.

Ray swatted his lower lip with his fingers and then ran them across the arm of Jerry's starched white short-sleeve shirt, eliciting a choice epithet from him as Ray lifted his headset and scanned the monitors for updates.

With the passengers finally off on their EVA tour, Ray hoped he could finally have a few words alone with Caitlin. He spoke into his headset. "Hey, sweetheart."

"How's it going, honeybunch?" came the reply, a falsetto impersonation of a female voice.

"That's slap-on-the-knee funny, Dallas. You learn that one in medical school or astronaut school?"

"Clown school, Bozo. Now, what may I do for you?"

Ray smiled despite himself. "You may patch me through to Caitlin, that's what you may do for me, Dallas."

There was a pause before Dallas responded, "Sorry, no can do, Ray. Caitlin was ordered on the EVA tour by Big Boss Blake. I can put you through, but you're going to be whispering sweet nothings into seven pairs of ears instead of one. And that's assuming I don't eavesdrop, which is one mighty risky assumption."

Ray swallowed hard, wishing he hadn't had that pint of Dos Equis with his meal. Now he was as parched as he was anxious. What the hell did Blake bring Caitlin on the EVA tour for? Surely, the prick wouldn't think of setting foot near those caverns he'd heard mentioned.

Ray suddenly turned serious. "Dallas, can you still see the group outside the LEM?"

"That's a negative, Ray-Ray. The group's out on the rovers."

"Rovers?" Ray felt his lunch coming up for air and quickly swallowed it back down. "What fucking rovers? I didn't hear anything about any rovers."

"Oh, right," Dallas said with a chuckle. "I realize you wannabe gods on the ground like to know whether we astronauts wipe our asses with three sheets or four, but Big Boss Blake likes his secrets and today those secrets got wheels. We brought two rovers with us. *Suuuurprise.*"

Ray felt a strong urge to put his fist through the closest monitor. *Fucking Blake.*

"Dallas, listen. Where did they go?"

"Mission Control, this is Command Module *Certainty*, over."

Paul's voice froze Ray for an instant, then: "Go ahead, *Certainty*. Over."

"Kindly shut the fuck up. I'm trying to catch a little shut-eye up here, over."

Flustered, Ray nearly flung his headset across the room.

"Hey, take a look at this." Jerry jerked his head toward his computer display.

"Not now, Fat Boy. Mind your monitors."

"Got some local weather. Real sudden. Weird looking, though. You should see this."

Ray leaned closer to Jerry's workstation while he took a moment to regain his composure. *All right, McCullough, this ain't your first rodeo...* He continued monitoring the radio channel while he stared at a radar map on Jerry's screen. He pointed at an unusual signature and shot Jerry a quizzical expression. *What is that?*

"Not sure yet, but it just cropped up a few minutes ago. Whatever it is, it's heading right for the Spaceport. I'll see what I can find out." Jerry began to peck away at his keyboard. Ray looked over his shoulder as Jerry worked, squinting and leaning forward to be closer to the screen.

"Say, Jer, what's that?"

The big man continued hammering at the keys. "What's what?"

"That file right there. I don't recognize that icon."

"Huh?" Jerry's fingers froze over the keyboard.

"That one." Ray reached out and hovered his pointer finger over the file shortcut. Jerry turned around to look at him.

"I don't know. You looking for a new game or something to kill some time, or should we get back to tracking this huge freaking storm that's barreling down on us?"

Ray grinned. "Yeah, yeah, I hear you, but humor me a second, would you? I've never seen that type of file here before. Just open it, what's the big deal?"

"Fine. Probably just some useless sys-admin utility no one ever—" Jerry choked off mid-sentence as a video application opened in a small window in the center of the screen. "Well that's strange, I never—"

Ray's fingers tightened around the top of Jerry's chair back as a grainy color video started to play. The distinctive gray shades of the moon were immediately recognizable to both men, even without the astronaut in center frame. He stooped low as he walked, careful to avoid bumping his head on the low ceiling....

"There's a ceiling there!" Ray noted. "And look at the date stamp on this. That was Flight 17, let's see, who was on that...."

Suddenly on screen the astronaut turned around and his name was visible stenciled on his suit. KNOWLES.

"Strat Knowles? I don't believe he was on Flight 17." Jerry's features screwed up into a mask of confusion.

Ray nodded slowly as it dawned on him they were looking at a video of a previous Outer Limits moon voyage they had never been made privy to. "That's because this isn't Flight 17. But it's not Flight 18 either. Call it Flight 17 B."

"Never heard of that one."

"Me neither, Jerry! That's because there wasn't one. But something tells me we're looking at it right now."

Jerry swiveled in his chair to look at Ray. "And what happened to Strat? He's not with us anymore."

"That's right. He retired right after Flight 17, supposedly, although this doesn't appear to be Flight 17. To become a consultant, is what I heard."

"Going for the big bucks, huh?"

Ray smiled. "That's right. Blake hired Caitlin right after he left." *Thank God for that, no more lonely nights in the desert.*

Then the movie commanded their attention as, on screen, the wall next to the astronaut appeared to dissolve and then reform as if in motion. "What in the..." Jerry started. But then the screen exploded in hectic static, so bright it hurt their eyes. When it resolved about fifteen seconds later, KNOWLES was no longer standing. In fact, he was barely in the frame at all anymore, except for his blood, that is. They could see copious splashes of it on the tunnel walls, which had somehow reformed, or perhaps the angle of the shot had changed during the intervening static.

The two controllers were silent for a few moments as they struggled to comprehend what was going on, what had transpired.

"It looked like Strat..." Jerry started but couldn't finish.

"Like he was killed by something in those caves?"

Before Jerry could answer, an alarm rang and a red flashing icon came to life on Jerry's monitor. "Severe Weather Alert. It's getting worse. We've got to check this out." He closed out of the video and brought up the Doppler radar view, where an amorphous blob stretched across the desert.

But although Ray knew that the approaching system, whatever it was, was significant, there was only one thing on his mind. He patted Jerry on the shoulder. "Good work. I've got to make a call up to the LEM." He turned and strode back to his communications console. He picked up the transmitter and addressed Dallas.

"Did Garner tell you where the group was heading?"

"Affirmative, Ray-Ray. Your sweetheart's leading them over to McMurdo Crater. We missed our designated landing mark, but the rov—"

Ray glanced over at Jerry, now preoccupied with his weird radar. "Dallas, switch to Q-Comm, please."

Ray switched over, waited briefly while Dallas did the same.

Dallas, suddenly serious: "What is it, Ray?"

"I need you to bring her back for me?"

"Who? Caitlin?"

"Yeah, get her back to the LEM. I don't give a fuck how. Tell her you need her help to program the diagnostics or to check out some program alarm."

"Seriously, Ray?"

"I don't give a shit what you tell her, Dallas. Just get her back to the damn LEM and do it now."

When Ray turned, Jerry and another two controllers who happened to be walking past were staring at him as though he'd just taken a shit on Blake Garner's fajitas.

"All right, all right," Dallas came back. "Let's not get those panties in a bunch. Stand by."

"Standing by." Ray kicked his chair over and shouted, *"What the fuck y'all looking at?* Get back to work or you can take your resumes to fucking NASA and fart around with simulations or robots the rest of your lives. And find out whatever the hell that is on that radar!"

"Ray," Dallas came back.

"Go ahead, Dallas."

"I'll keep trying, but I'm not getting anyone on EVA comm at the moment."

Ray pressed his right hand against his headset to keep it from trembling. But when he spoke, his lip was going. "Why the hell not, Dal?"

Ray didn't need to hear the LEM pilot's reply.

"My guess is that they went down to explore the crater and there's too much rock to transmit through down there."

Jerry called over to Ray as soon as he set down the transmitter. "Hey, I've got a match for that radar signature."

Ray looked over at him, glad for anything to distract him from worrying about Caitlin. There was nothing he could do for her at the moment.

"So what is it?"

"Dust storm. Huge one! Coming our way."

15 | BELOW

James Burton had never known himself to be claustrophobic. Yet as he walked through the narrowing cavern, he felt his pulse quicken, his lungs working to take deeper, longer breaths. On either side of him the walls of rock appeared as though they were about to reach out and grab his arms. He imagined the floor of the cavern melting around his feet, pulling him under like quicksand. Even the ceiling, which was well above their heads and seemingly stable, looked to him like it was made of snow and could succumb to a cave-in at any given second.

In front of James, Asami Imura remained enthralled. As she studied the rock formations, she spoke aloud, uttering suppositions, muttering something about the *subterranean regolith*, predicting what they would find next. Her voice put him at ease. Somewhat.

When they finally reached a fork in the tunnels, Blake interrupted Asami and said, "Okay, here's what we're going to do…" He outlined a plan.

"You're splitting us up?" James asked once Blake finished giving instructions. Burton didn't sound frightened – on the contrary, more like puzzled. But only for a moment. Only until he went through the two teams in his head.

Caitlin Swain would lead Asami and James.

Blake would lead Martin Hughes and Suzette Calderon.

He was readying them for a discovery of some sort. Wanted to make sure the moment was captured by cameras when he was there. Having Suzette on his team would allow him as many "takes" as he needed.

No "One small step for man" on this journey. Blake was hell bent on getting this right. The world would see and hear exactly what he wanted them to, would remember this moment precisely how he wanted them to.

The billionaire explorer said, "Caitlin, you'll lead Team One through the tunnel on the right. The tunnels merge again in about eight hundred feet. I'll lead Team Two through the left tunnel, and we'll switch on the return trip."

"Aye, sir," Swain said.

"Ready?" Blake said to Martin after the first team disappeared.

The exobiologist smiled under his helmet. "You bet your life, old boy."

There was no discussion about switching frequencies. The two teams needed to remain in touch at all times. So James continued to listen to Suzette prattle on about flattering angles and ideal backgrounds while she, Blake and Hughes traveled through the left corridor. In the other tunnel, James' team, led by Caitlin, remained silent. He soon learned that in addition to recording this event, Suzette was required to do a bit of playacting as well. A few gasps of wonderment and awe for the sake of Outer Limits and Team One.

James' headlamp lit his way while Caitlin and Asami forged on up ahead of him. His eyes were trained on the floor because it may have been that they were playing tricks on him again, as they had on the surface. The ground seemed unsteady beneath his feet. Not quite unstable, but...

Suddenly, Blake Garner's voice was shouting in his ears. "Suzette! *Stay with the group.*"

The videographer replied in her usual tone. "I just need some shots of this."

Then Asami: "What the hell *is* that?" James looked at that unsteady ground again. Was that what she was talking about?

Blake again: "Suzette, this is the last time I'm going to warn you. *Remain with the group.*"

Hughes' voice suddenly cut in. "Good god!"

"Rethinking things, Martin?" Blake taunted.

"It's an expression, you idiot." James made a mental note of the short fuses everyone seemed to have as soon as they entered the tunnels.

Up ahead somewhere out of sight, Blake and Hughes had stopped. They stood in front of a sloping wall. Over their shoulders James could just make out what looked like a large opening in the rock.

"Your crew did this, right, Blake?" Hughes asked.

Blake didn't respond. Something had apparently caused Hughes not to follow the script.

As James reached them, the biologist was shrugging Blake's arm off his shoulder. "Fuck off," Hughes said. "You're a goddamn liar, Bla—"

Hughes' voice suddenly cut out, and all James could hear was Suzette's. She was speaking quickly, rattling off words like a machine gun. Describing something very similar to what stood before them—some inexplicable opening in the rock wall.

"Suzette!" Blake shouted again. "We can't *see* you. Return to the team, *now*."

Suzette continued her frantic description as James peered into the hole in the side of the tunnel.

"...appears that the rock was smashed, or perhaps *drilled* here...from the inside out."

16 | LIGHTS, CAMERA...

Caitlin did her best to sound authoritative while her voice wavered. "Suzette, I can't see you yet, but step back from the opening. The ground may not be stable." Up ahead, the marketing VP continued to aim a video camera into the hole in the tunnel wall.

A spot of light moved erratically to Caitlin's right and James Burton loped his way up to her. She couldn't hear his footfalls—there was no sound on the moon other than through their communications channels due to the absence of air—but when his headlamp remained fixed on the same spot of tunnel wall, she knew he had reached her. He said nothing. Their FAA chaperone was turning out to be quite a cool customer for a first-time lunar visitor who was usually bound to a desk, Caitlin thought. For that she was grateful.

Aside from Suzette, it was actually Asami who gave her cause for concern. Though she'd been to the moon before, this was her first trek inside the tunnels, as it was for all of them except for Blake. The moon scientist was in an almost trance-like stupor as she meandered up to Caitlin and James, hypothesizing aloud to no one in particular about the extensive subterranean channels.

"I would say they remind me of lava tubes. Ancient lava tubes that once contained hot magma during young Luna's volcanically active beginnings, but so far I haven't seen any flow lines on the walls to indicate a drained tube..." Asami's suited hand trailing along the tunnel wall took over as her voice trailed off. "It's also unusual that I haven't seen any traces of mineral deposits in the walls, given that—"

Caitlin interrupted her. "Dr. Imura, I'm sorry, but right now we need to focus on getting our group back together."

"Certainly. My apologies," Asami said. The beam from her headlamp bounced around the ceiling, but she stopped talking.

Then Blake's voice cut through everything. "Suzette! Did I hear you say you were taking video? Turn it off, now. Now! Is that clear?"

Silence.

"Suzette, acknowledge at once!" Still no reply. Caitlin could hear Blake and Martin speaking to one another in hushed tones. She couldn't help but strain to hear...*What is that...stop stepping on my foot!*

"Caitlin, I need you to handle this!" Blake's demanding tone drowned out all other conversation and snapped Caitlin to attention.

"I'm almost to her, sir." Caitlin put her hand behind her, palm out, warning Asami and James to stay back while she followed the tunnel's curve to the left. The ceiling here was lower by a couple of feet, forcing Caitlin to stoop as she came to what was obviously the opening of which Suzette had spoken. A narrow tunnel continued left and wound around a rocky promontory that divided Caitlin's tunnel from the one where Blake's team was. On her right side the tunnel wall was marred by a jagged hole thrust through it.

"Suzette?" she transmitted. Their marketing exec wasn't in front of the hole in the wall, which Caitlin recognized immediately from Suzette's harried description. *It does look like something drilled through this wall from the other side.*

"Blake, is Suzette with Team One?" She could picture the girl hunched obliviously over her computer, thinking she could get out one of her vapid messages to whatever social media site was in fashion these days through the walls of these tunnels. *Not gonna happen.*

She heard a groundswell of chatter, mostly indistinguishable. *...do you mean...how did I know? ...a box!*

"Blake?" What was going on over there?

"Caitlin, *no*, Suzette is not here, over."

Goosebumps travelled up Caitlin's legs and arms as she looked back to the hole in the wall. She stepped closer to it. It didn't lead straight back more than a few feet, but went down. With great care and while calling out Suzette's name, Caitlin eased onto her hands and knees. She crawled to the entrance, where a few larger rocks jutted up through the rim of the opening like crooked incisors in a gaping mouth. Careful to avoid them, Caitlin stuck her neck through the hole. Nowhere to go but down, although the hole widened the deeper it got. And then she saw it.

Suzette's video camera, lying on the ground about ten feet below. Its own light source fanned out across the tunnel floor, illuminating a greater swath of the chamber than Caitlin's piercing but narrow headlamp beam. At the outer edges of the camera's light, Caitlin saw movement. It wasn't Suzette, but in the back of her mind she realized she was still calling her name.

The ground itself was moving, rolling.

17 | ... REACTION

Caitlin backed away from the hole and stood. When she turned around, Asami and James were rounding the corner.

"Did Suzette go though there?" Asami asked, pointing into the ragged passage.

"Not sure yet. It leads straight down. Asami, James, I need you to follow me, please."

James silently nodded his helmet up and down.

"Sure," Asami said, still eyeing the hole. "You know, that doesn't really look like geological upheaval," she said, starting to walk over to it. "Was there any kind of digging or drilling activity by Outer Limits on the earlier missions? Because I could swear—"

"There wasn't," Caitlin said. "There were some preliminary tunnel walks like we're doing now, that's what I was—"

Caitlin cut herself off as Martin Hughes' voice trilled in his upper registers. "What the fuck *is* that, Blake? If this is some kind of hoax it is not the least bit amusing."

"It's not a hoax."

"Then what *is* it?"

"That's what I was hoping you could tell me," Blake said. "You're the exobiologist."

Caitlin, James and Asami stared for a moment at their own space-suited reflections in each other's helmets before Caitlin took the lead into the tunnel that led around the corner to the one Blake's team was in.

"Blake, Caitlin here: Team Two is on the way to join you at your location with information, over." *With information* was an Outer Limits code phrase that meant, *we need to switch to a secure channel to discuss an issue not meant for outside ears.* Not that

Burton wasn't already aware Suzette was missing, but still. She knew Blake would want privacy while they figured out how to deal with it.

Caitlin reached for the volume control to her earpiece as static crackled over the comm channel, probably because of the thick rock wall separating them. She heard Blake say, "...saw them once before but I...astrobiologist..."

Caitlin strode as fast as she dared, careful not to hit her head on the ceiling, while gesturing for James and Asami to follow her. They rounded the end of the rocky wall that separated their tunnels. She sidestepped around a jumble of loose rock on the tunnel floor and entered the stretch of tunnel where Blake's team was supposed to be. She intended to interrupt whatever the hell they were doing; this was no time for courtesy. But she was not prepared for what she saw here.

Blake and Martin stood facing one another about four feet apart. Martin's helmet light reflected off Blake's faceplate in a brilliant starburst of light. But it wasn't Blake's head Caitlin was looking at.

His hands were held out in front of him, cupped together. In them, something squirmed and wriggled. Caitlin was still too far away to discern any detail. Whatever it was, it had the unwavering attention of both Martin and Blake, neither of whom appeared entirely comfortable with it. Martin shifted his weight from one foot to the other, as if ready to put distance between himself and Blake at any second, but unsure of which direction in which to go.

Whatever was going on was far too bizarre for Caitlin to make sense of immediately and she needed to act now. "Blake, listen to me." She gave him a hand signal that meant to switch to a private channel. Blake either ignored her or didn't see it, because he continued his animated conversation with Martin.

"Just look at it! It's harmless, at least with your suit on."

"I really don't recommend coming into contact with it even through a suit, Blake. Whatever it is—"

To hell with the private channel, Caitlin thought. "BLAKE! SUZETTE IS MISSING!"

Blake slid one of his feet back on the tunnel floor as he crouched down and scooped up some dust in one hand while bobbling the object in his other.

"They get nervous without the dust," he said, pouring the regolith onto the thing, which appeared to be moving, but it was difficult for Caitlin to be sure because Blake himself was also in motion, in some kind of lunar balancing act. "Almost like a fish out of water," Blake continued, dumping more gray dust onto his cupped hand until it was full and rained in slow motion from his gloved fingers back to the cave floor.

"*Blake*, her camera is lying on the floor of a tunnel below us, and I saw the floor *move!*" At this, Martin looked away from the spectacle of Blake and the thing and turned toward Caitlin.

"I hear you, Caitlin," Blake said, his face unreadable behind his helmet.

"Maybe we should split up and go looking for her," Martin suggested.

"No splitting up." Blake reached into a vest pocket of his suit. The motion threw him off balance and he almost fell over as he juggled the object in his palm. "Martin, reach into my front left chest pocket, please, and pull out the sample container."

"I think you should let it go, Blake," Martin said. "We're not properly equipped for live biological specimen collection. We'll need to—"

"Whoa, wait a minute, did you just say 'live biological specimen?'" Asami asked, rounding the rock wall into view. "What *is* that in your hand, Blake?"

"This, my friends, is E. fucking T. The first ever extraterrestrial life, documented and witnessed by scientific professionals on this very mission. And it appears to be multi-cellular at that. All of you are making history."

"Suzette?" Caitlin reminded Blake.

"Let's go down into the cave you found and get her," Blake said. Martin reached a hand into Blake's suit pocket and removed a clear plastic cube. He stepped back from Blake and turned the container over in his hands.

"Put some dust in it," Blake said, before adding, "Caitlin, please take your team into the tunnel to get Suzette. We will be right behind you."

Martin knelt and put the cube to the ground. "This doesn't look like any bio-specimen container I've ever seen, Blake," he said, dragging the box through the lunar dust.

"About two-thirds full," Blake said, before addressing Caitlin. "Go now, Caitlin!"

The astronaut fought an upwelling of mixed emotions raging inside her. Blake had found some kind of life on the moon! She wanted to revel in the moment, to reflect on what this milestone meant for her life and career, and indeed, for humanity, but there was not time. She turned and headed back toward the mysterious opening.

Asami skipped after her, saying, "You said you saw the floor move. Could be a moonquake, although that thought is less than comforting down here. But seismic activity is quite common on the moon, and some quakes would register a 5.5 on our Richter scale back on Earth."

"It's for geologic specimens," Blake said as Martin rose to his feet, "but it's airtight, it has a locking lid, it's sturdy and it's chemically inert."

"And it's all we've got, right?" Martin said, walking over to Blake with the dust-filled cube.

"Right."

"All right, I'm on board. I would give my left nut to get some DNA from this thing. If it has DNA. Drop the critter in." Martin held the cube poised beneath Blake's hand.

"I'd like to go back to the lander now," James announced. He stood motionless behind Asami, where he'd been silently observing the goings on for some time.

At this, Caitlin turned around in time to see Blake fumble the creature as he looked up at James. Martin deftly maneuvered the container in time to catch it, snapping the lid down with soundless finality. She saw Blake nod thanks to Martin while a flurry of soil roiled inside the acrylic cube like a dust devil in miniature.

"Is something wrong, James? We need to find Suzette now." Blake took the specimen in its cube from Martin and placed it carefully into his own suit pocket.

"I don't need to go cave exploring anymore," James replied, his voice low and calm. "I came this far, I saw this much, and that's enough for me. Earlier you told me that anytime anyone wanted to go back to the lander, for any reason, that you would have Caitlin escort them back. You said that's how the tourist trips will work, too. So, let's see it. I want to go back now. "

18 | LIFE

Although James was glad to shake Blake up with his request to go back to the rover, the singular thought continuously refreshing itself in his mind was that writhing animal thing. *That's not microbial!* A lot of people expected the discovery of life outside Earth to be first seen under a microscope. He wasn't sure what the hell this thing was, that was for sure; he was no scientist. But he knew a wiggling animal when he saw one.

He could barely pay attention to the outrage expressed by Martin Hughes after being blindsided by Blake's find. Apparently Blake knew about these...creatures...from previous trips up here and had suppressed the news thus far, saving it for when he would have the corroboration of top scientists. *I can't wait to put this in my report.* But even James knew the stunning implications of the find.

That's not microscopic. A full-on animal found living on the moon!

He tried to tune out Blake and Caitlin arguing as he thought about it while both teams made their way through the tunnels.

Whatever it was, it was alive. The entity was either worm or insect or something in between.

But how? There's no atmosphere here on the moon.

That didn't change the facts, though. In Blake's possession was a life form from another world. He couldn't yet fathom the implications, not just for how people regarded the moon and taking trips to it, but for how our species regarded Earth – and itself.

What else might reside in these subterranean walls?

"Caitlin," Blake said into his comm unit, "meet me at the outside entrance to the tunnels."

"Blake," she protested, "I'm not going anywhere until we find Suzette."

Suzette. That's right. Blake's VP of Marketing had gone missing somewhere in the next tunnel over. That would absolutely have to find its way into his report, too, Burton thought. No doubt the walls were simply too thick in some areas to communicate via the radios. *How far could she have wandered off?*

"We are going to find Suzette," Blake said. "But first, we are going to escort Mr. Burton to the surface per his deliberately untimely request. Then you are going to drive him in a rover back to the LEM while Asami, Martin and I go back to get Suzette."

As James, Asami and Caitlin moved through the tunnel, James again felt out of breath. *Maybe that's why you asked to leave the tunnels? Maybe you really are scared? Can't hack it anymore?* He turned to check his oxygen gauge. When he did, his headlamp shone on the wall to his right. The rock appeared to shift ever so slightly. *Seeing things. Gotta get out of here before I pass out.*

When he reached the exit to the parallel tunnels, Blake and Martin were already there, standing on the crater's interior slope. Behind his helmet, Burton's eyes narrowed while he waited for Blake to meet his stare. Instead, Blake simply offered his hand. "James, we'll see you back at the LEM."

Burton shook his hand but didn't say anything as Blake walked around to the exit of the other tunnel, Martin Hughes trailing him by several feet. Just up ahead a single headlamp beamed in their direction. Blake waved at it.

"Asami, lead us to the spot where you last saw Suzette."

19 | CAR TROUBLE

Outside of the tunnel, Caitlin picked her way toward the crater's rim. After the darkness of the subterranean labyrinth, the glare of the sun off the moon's surface was as brilliant as a ski slope on the brightest of days. Still, she was glad to be out of the dungeon-like environment. Glad, that is, except for the company of James Burton. He was doing a weird sideways hopping move as opposed to Caitlin's steady long strides, but it was getting him up the crater.

"Everything seems okay with your suit, Mr. Burton. You feel okay? Claustrophobic down there? You can answer truthfully, they can't hear us over the comm, it doesn't penetrate underground."

"Nah, I was fine. I wanted to prove a point to Blake that it's not as simple as it seems to give people the choice of leaving once they get so far from the LEM, especially underground."

Caitlin stopped her forward progress about twenty feet from the crater rim. She grabbed Burton's arm as he went hopping past and turned him back toward her.

"You *asshole*! Suzette is missing down there! We should both be searching for her. This is not the time to try and prove some petty point. I'm going back down and you're coming with me."

"Take it easy. I'm exaggerating a little. It's not like I had to go running out of there or anything, but I have no interest in exploring the tunnels. It wasn't even in the itinerary. And that strange life down there—"

"Blake wanted it to be a surprise."

"He certainly succeeded on that score. Even the exobiologist didn't seem too happy about being taken for a loop like that. I was surprised Blake brought us all down there. Let him be surprised that I wanted to leave early." Burton hopped off again, breaking free from Caitlin's grip as he bounded toward the rim. Caitlin started after him.

"It was a mistake for Blake to even allow you to escort me out of here alone," Burton continued.

"Why is that?" Caitlin swallowed hard as the Earth came into view above the crater rim. *Ray...*

"What if I just completely freaked out? Could you really control me? I must outweigh you by a good fifty pounds!"

"Stop it, Mr. Burton, you're scaring me."

"Well, think about it! Suppose I'm Joe Tourist and I've come this far but all of a sudden I'm not comfortable anymore and I just...WANT TO GO BACK HOME!"

Caitlin winced in pain with Burton's sudden yelling and clawed at her comm unit's volume control. "What the hell's the matter with you?" she said but she was drowned out by Burton, who now pointed at the Earth, screaming, "TAKE ME HOME! I WANT TO GO NOW, WANNA GO RIGHT FUCKING NOW TAKE ME HOME!" He jumped up and down, rising high in the weak gravity before landing again, sending a loose jumble of gray rocks and soil sliding a little ways down the crater.

Caitlin hurried past Burton to the lip of the crater. "Are you done?" she asked when he stopped yelling.

"I think I've made my point."

"We have psych tests to predict that kind of behavior in potential clients. You took them yourself."

"Easy to fake your way through. And not only that, but they can be plain wrong. Psychology is certainly not what you would call an exact science. In fact, some would argue it's not really a science at all."

"Just don't do anything like that again, okay? You've made enough points for one afternoon. I won't—holy *shit*...." She paused, staring down the outside of the crater.

"What is it? What's the matter?" Alarm crept into Burton's voice as he moved to Caitlin's side. When an astronaut said, *holy shit*, it wasn't going to be a good thing. But then he thought about it..."Oh, wait... I see. Good one! Giving me a little scare back, are you? Fair enough."

Caitlin swung her helmet side to side, pointing down the crater. "We're missing a rover."

Burton followed her finger with his eyes until he spotted the lone moon buggy parked about twenty feet down from the rim. "What? Where is it?"

"Down there," Caitlin said, pointing all the way to the crater's base, where the other vehicle lay on its side.

"My God. How did that happen?"

Caitlin almost told Burton about how she had placed the wheel chocks, but decided she didn't want to give him any more ammo against Blake. Maybe she hadn't been careful enough about it because Blake was rushing her back into the crater, Burton would allege. This was bad enough.

"Got me. It rolled down the crater, obviously. Some loose rock must have slipped out from under the wheels, disturbed by our passage, I guess. Let's ride this one down and check it out."

Caitlin climbed into the rover behind the joystick control. James walked around to the other side while Caitlin's earpiece crackled with Dallas' voice.

"Well, hello again, darlin'. Good to have you back in comm range. Everything copacetic, over?"

"I copy you, Dallas. Switch to Q-band, please, over." James would know she'd just went to a private channel with Dallas, but that was too bad. She made the frequency change while the FAA man took a seat beside her. She ignored his look and put the rover into gear.

"What's up?" Dallas asked. "How was the crater?"

"Lot going on, Dallas, and most of it not good. Burton and I are taking one of the rovers back to the LEM now. The others are still in the tunnels. Blake discovered some kind of small life form and he and Martin captured it in a specimen box. Also, Suzette—"

"Say again, Caitlin? *Life*?"

As she drove down the crater's outer slope, Caitlin recounted events for Dallas.

"You did the right thing," he said when she finished. "If somebody says they want to go back to the LEM, take them back to the LEM. Even if they say they're joking. It's nothing to mess with. Blake will find Suzette. She's probably updating her social network status with how we go to the bathroom up here or something like that."

Caitlin laughed out loud as she leveled out the rover after navigating around a large boulder. James pointed wordlessly off to their right.

"I can see the other rover now," Caitlin said to Dallas.

"Before you switch back to the party channel, I promised Ray that I'd relay his message to you, although it's too late now, anyway."

Caitlin's breath caught at the mention of Ray's name. She stole a glance at her home planet before returning her attention to the lunar terrain beneath her wheels. "What'd he say?"

"He said to get you back to the LEM as soon as possible, that you should stay out of the tunnels. Sounded highly concerned. Something I don't know about?"

Caitlin pulled up to Blake's rover, wondering how Ray could have known about those living things in the tunnels. Or maybe it was just general concern about doing a subterranean EVA so far from the LEM?

The rover lay on its side, two of its wheels still spinning with no air resistance to counteract their motion. "Tell him I'm heading back to the lander, and I'm fine. First, I'm going to check out Blake's rover, see if it's salvageable."

She pulled her rover to a stop and walked to the overturned moon buggy. She felt her stomach clench as she surveyed the damage. It wasn't good. The battery casing had cracked, and she could see flammable electrolyte leaking into the lunar soil. *Great. We're polluting the moon already.* The electrical wires leading from the battery had been ripped from their connections. Even worse, the rear axle and been severely bent.

Caitlin was about to speak over the common frequency when an anomaly on the moon's surface caught her eye. It was in the distance, about halfway between the wrecked rover and... the other LEM. Black Sky's lander. She focused on the object for a bit and saw that it was really two objects. Bouncing, moving. Hopping.

Spacesuits!

Two space-suited figures were making their way toward the Black Sky LEM.

Caitlin's blood ran as cold as the space around her. She looked back up the crater, carefully examining the ground. There! Extra sets of boot prints.

"What's wrong?" James asked, watching her silently gaze up the hill.

Could it be that the Black Sky team had deliberately sabotaged their rover, and tried to make it look like an accident? If they hadn't come out of the tunnels early, after all, those two people would probably be back at that LEM and she wouldn't have thought to look around for the footprints...

She cautioned herself not to voice this concern to Mr. Burton. Not now. *Way* too much going on. She could give him the other known issue, though, that he would be confronted with sooner or later.

"Just thinking about our rover situation, James. Axle's shot, battery's shot. This thing isn't going anywhere and I'm afraid my Triple-A membership expired."

Dallas' voice came over the private frequency. "Get your asses back to the LEM, Caitlin. Meanwhile, I'll be thinking about how to solve our problem."

"What problem is that?" Caitlin asked him.

Dallas replied, "How to transport six people in a four-person lunar vehicle. Because the oxygen supplies in your suits won't last long enough to walk back to the LEM." After a slight pause, he came back. "Looking on the bright side, if you can't find Suzette, it'll only be five people in a four-person vehicle."

Caitlin shook her head, aware that James was watching her. "Not funny, Dallas. Not funny at all."

20 | FOUND FOOTAGE

Asami Imura clipped one end of a climbing rope to a special harness on her spacesuit. She handed Blake the other end. "I'm counting on you to belay me, Blake. Don't get distracted by anything, okay?"

Blake gave her an okay hand signal since they couldn't read each other's eyes through the helmet visors. He knew her command wasn't insubordination. They were both rock climbers, and he knew that's where she was coming from. Safety first. "What, me mess up the first ever rock climb on the moon, you've got to be kidding? Steady as she goes." He took the rope and threaded it through his own harness.

"Be careful down there," Martin Hughes felt the need to add, gazing down at the fallen video camera from a safe distance away from the edge.

"I will be." Asami backed up to the opening in the wall and leaned back, testing the rope with Blake's grip.

"This is much easier than it is on Earth!" The entrepreneur held up the rope in one hand as if to demonstrate this fact.

"Fractional gravity or not, Blake, please watch what you're doing. Here I go."

Asami jumped into the hole, sliding down the rope and pushing off the cave wall once with her feet on the way down. She landed in a crouch nearby the camera.

"I'm on the ground. Okay so far."

She stood fully upright and turned around in a slow circle, assessing her new surroundings.

"You see her?" Blake wanted to know.

"Negative. Small chamber, too, and I don't see any outlets at all...it's just this one room. The way I came in is the only entrance or exit."

"What? That's impossible! Check again." Blake's voice was edgy.

"Will do." Asami walked the perimeter of the subterranean cavern, paying close attention to the walls and floor to be certain she wasn't overlooking a small passageway. But by the time she had walked all four walls, she had still found no other way out. She informed Blake of this fact.

"Check the camera, then. I told her not to film but I'm guessing she did anyway. Maybe it'll show what she saw right before she dropped it."

Asami went to the video recorder and picked it up. She played back its images, soundless due to the lack of air, and watched.

The point-of-view was from Susan herself, occasionally showing her other gloved hand in the foreground as she aimed the lens. For the first few seconds, the video showed the same environs Asami now found herself in. But soon things changed. The camera view became unsteady, as though Susan were struggling to keep her balance. And then the floor itself yawned open, revealing a throat-like passage into which Suzette floated along with a shower of swirling dust particles.

"Asami, what's on the camera?" Blake sounded impatient as always, but the moon scientist was having trouble processing what she was looking at. How could this be? It looked from the footage as though the marketing exec had simply been swallowed up by the floor. A sudden and severe moonquake, or cave collapse?

Asami tore her gaze from the camera's display to examine the actual ground beneath her feet. *It is ground, right?* Bending down to touch the chamber floor through her gloved hand, the selenologist sensed something wasn't quite right about it. It didn't have the rock-solid feel that moon *rocks* should have. Not only that, she thought, studying the striations—*(more like patterns)* in the floor—*they don't really look like*...but she never completed that thought.

The cave floor moved. She steadied herself, to be certain, and waited. There it came again. It *moved*. She considered that she was lightheaded from lack of oxygen, but a quick check of her gauges showed this not to be true. *The ground is moving.*

As she began to voice her concern to Blake and Martin, her feet started wobbling even though she was not moving them. She screamed into her transmitter. "Blake pull me up! Up now!"

At that moment the ground parted beneath her feet—opened up completely—and she started falling. She looked down to see how far she had to fall, but it was too dark to see past the...*what is that?* A glistening, slimy cavern, sort of like a raspy tongue with row upon row of tooth-like structures. Moving, like a swallowing throat. And she was dropping straight into it, too stunned to even utter Blake's name again.

She felt a harsh tug on her midsection as Blake jerked upward on the rope and she began to float up through the bizarre cavity into which she had fallen. Wet, organized structure passed before her eyes in a dizzying array of patterns and motion.

And then she was in the chamber again, being raised through it by Blake's climbing rope. Walls. Normal-looking. Unmoving. Dry, like the moon should always be. But looking back down one last time before she was yanked through that strange hole in the wall, Asami saw the soaked, moving structure drop lower into the recesses from wherever it had come.

And then there was only a black hole.

21 | N̶O̶ ONE GETS LEFT BEHIND

"Maybe an earthquake? Moonquake, I mean," Blake speculated after hearing Asami's breathless account of what it was like down there in the moving cave.

"So it opened up the depths to reveal water, or at least liquid of some kind?" Martin asked, peering down into the chamber. "Hey, it looks like things stopped moving around down there."

Blake, Asami and Martin all gazed into the chamber, which was in fact now still, but with a deeper floor than before. Blake checked his suit gauges. "Our oxygen supply is getting low enough that we should start heading back to the LEM." He received no arguments, and the trio began making their way out of the tunnel system.

They moved quickly through the underground labyrinth, Blake by now sure of the way back. As they moved they transmitted to Suzette, calling her name, but no response was received. All of them kept their eyes open for signs of movement from the tunnel itself, but saw nothing of the kind by the time they reached the exit to the underground system. They huddled at the rocky outcropping on the crater's inside slope. Left unspoken was the gravity of what they were faced with: leaving Suzette behind somewhere in the tunnels.

"One last try, then we go," Blake said. They transmitted her name a few more times. Blake added, "Suzette: for some reason if you can hear us but can't talk back—malfunctioning transmitter, perhaps—know this: we *are* coming back for you. We *will* find you."

Neither Asami nor Martin said anything. They both knew that should Suzette actually be faced with the horror of being trapped somewhere in a rockslide or tunnel collapse, with a radio that would receive but not transmit, she'd be on the brink of insanity right about now, if not actually over it.

Blake shook them from their distressing reveries. "Let's get to the rover."

They trekked their way up the inside of the crater's slope, always wary of the ground, watching for movement. Upon reaching the lip, Blake stood and surveyed the view while Asami and Martin climbed up beside him.

"What the—" Blake cut himself off as he tried to make sense of what he was seeing. Or not seeing, as was the case.

"What's the matter?" Martin asked.

"There's only one rover here, and it's down there." Blake pointed to the wrecked moon buggy at the bottom of the outside of the crater.

"Caitlin took James back to the LEM in the other one," Martin reminded him.

"But something—" Blake broke off as he stared down at the remaining rover. "Let's just get down there."

"It looks like it rolled, is that what you were going to say?" Martin said, his voice wavering as he bounded down the crater's outer face.

No answer came, and when Martin turned to look at Blake, he saw his lips moving but heard nothing, meaning he was talking on a different channel, possibly to Caitlin or maybe to someone in the LEM. They continued down the slope toward the moon buggy. About halfway down, Caitlin's voice came over the common channel. "Blake, you hear me? I'm almost back to the LEM."

"Copy. What happened to my rover?"

"Don't want to discuss over open frequencies, switch to X-band, over."

Blake made an adjustment to his radio and then Martin couldn't hear the conversation. Caitlin told Blake on the private channel about her sighting of the two astronauts walking away from the rover toward the Black Sky lunar lander.

"Caitlin, listen to me. Does Dallas know about this yet?"

"Of course, Blake. He's the one who said it was a good thing I bring James back to the LEM, otherwise we all wouldn't fit in one rover."

"Tell him not to report on the rover crash to Mission Control, copy? And the official line on Suzette is that she is missing. We may still be able to find her. No outside communication regarding the matter until we have something conclusive, is that clear?"

A beat of silence ensued while Caitlin processed the fact that Blake was worried about his ever-important reputation. He was already in damage control mode.

"I said *is that clear?*"

"Sure, Blake. It's clear. That wasn't really on my mind, I have to say. We have an astronaut to find. Let's stay focused on that."

"Okay, switching back over to main channel..." As soon as they did they heard Martin's voice, a little higher pitched than usual.

"How are we going to get back to the LEM? The oxygen in our suits—"

Blake interrupted him. "We're working something out, Martin. Give us a second, please."

The voice of James Burton joined in. "Still think these moonwalks are tourist ready, do you, Blake?"

"Will you shut up already, Mr. Burton! You're part of the reason we're in this mess in the first place."

"Oh really? I don't see how the fact that one of your rovers rolled down the hill would have been changed if I hadn't asked to leave early. In fact, I may have actually *helped* you by giving you more time to fix the problem instead of finding out about it even later."

"Gentlemen, please," Martin soothed. "This is no place for an argument."

"I agree," Caitlin said. "Blake, as soon as I drop Mr. Burton off at the LEM, I'll turn right around and come back to the crater to pick up you, Asami and Martin. Just stay by the crashed rover, all right? Don't wander off. We're pulling up to the LEM now."

Blake gave the thumbs up signal to Martin and Asami while he replied. "Good. We'll be standing by the rover, over."

Caitlin clicked off and the three moonwalkers stared at each others' faceplate reflections for a moment, until Martin said, "So we have a bit of a wait for our ride. In the meantime, riddle me this: How do you think that life form we found..." He pointed to the bulge in Blake's spacesuit where he had stowed the specimen container. "...is able to stay alive in the complete absence of oxygen and water?"

Asami answered. "We'll have to analyze the chemical composition of the moon dust back in the lab. See exactly what it's made of. That might give us some clues."

"Agreed," Martin said with enthusiasm. He turned to Blake. "When we return to the LEM, I'd like to make use of the lab straight away to study the specimen."

"And I the rocks and soil samples, particularly the soil in the specimen container," Asami added.

The Outer Limits CEO stared blankly off in the direction of the Black Sky lander.

"Blake?" Asami jarred him from whatever thoughts he was having.

"Huh? Oh right. The lab. Sure, you can get right to work in there as soon as we get back."

"You don't sound all that excited, Blake, for a man poised to unlock the secrets of life in the universe, "Martin said.

Blake didn't turn away from his competitor's lander. "There are other secrets to unlock as well."

22 | GROUPTHINK

"Here she comes!" Asami pointed across the lunar plain at the clouds of dust kicked up by the moon buggy. They watched it draw near in silence, Blake having finally turned away from Black Sky's lander to join the conversation about the strange life form. He had the cube out with the creature, now hidden in the moon dust on the bottom, when Caitlin rolled to a stop a few feet from the group.

"Reminds me of waiting for the bus as a kid," Martin quipped as he hopped in back of the rover with Asami. Blake sat up front with Caitlin, but she remained at the wheel.

"How's your oh-two supply?" Caitlin greeted them with. A chorus of low readings ensued. Caitlin put the rover into gear and turned toward the LEM.

"And so how is our dear FAA representative doing now? Has he recovered from his frightful excursion?"

No one laughed. Caitlin replied. "It's not funny, Blake. I know he was being deliberately rash to try and prove a point, but if someone wants to go back to the LEM, we have to take them. You know that. Dallas agrees."

"We should conserve our oxygen by not talking," Blake returned.

They made the rest of the drive back to the LEM in silence. By the time they pulled up to the airlock ladder, Asami reported that her breaths were getting harder to pull.

Caitlin, who had swapped out for a fresh spacesuit oxygen unit after bringing Burton back, jumped from the rover and bunny-hopped over to the ladder. "C'mon. I'll get the airlock." She opened the outer door while the other three exited the rover and moved to the ladder. When they were all inside the airlock space,

Caitlin sealed the outer door and began the pressurization process. That completed, she removed her suit helmet, taking a few tentative breaths before a smile took over her features.

"C'mon in, the water's fine!" The others also removed their suits and then Caitlin led the way through the inner airlock door back into the lander's cabin.

Martin held his hands out to Blake. "Specimen, please. We'll need to get right to work on it in the lab."

Blake appeared to hesitate for a moment, but they could hear Dallas talking, and he handed it over before heading off in that direction. "Be careful with it!" he said as he walked away. Asami and Martin exchanged grins over the top of the acrylic cube. Two scientists with an alien life form to play with! They headed for the portion of the spacecraft that held the tiny laboratory.

#

Blake, Caitlin, Dallas and James huddled in the control alcove. Before Blake could take over, Dallas shot Caitlin a look and said, "Ray wants you to call him, right now."

Caitlin turned on a heel and started for another part of the ship. Blake called after her, "Do not mention Suzette!"

James watched her walk away and then turned back to Blake and Dallas.

"Excuse me, Mr. Burton?" Blake said.

"Yes?" He turned to face Blake.

"Can you give us a moment of privacy, please?"

James' eyes narrowed. "Absolutely not! You should be discussing your missing astronaut, not wasting time worrying about the likes of me. This is going in my report!" Burton produced his notepad and began scribbling furiously.

"Asshole," Blake muttered under his breath.

James' pen stopped. "*What*?"

"Just something else for your report, I guess. Fine, stay here and be a distraction while I talk to Dallas."

The Lunar Module Pilot eyed both men in turn and then, realizing that Burton was going nowhere, addressed Blake in his presence. "There's something you should know about. Besides Suzette."

Blake visibly tensed. Even the problems had problems around here. "What is it?"

"I still haven't been able to fix the lander's guidance system, which I was hoping I might be able to complete while you were on your moonwalk."

"What's holding you back?"

James' eyes followed the exchange like a spectator at a ping pong match.

"Mission Control is helping me work out a solution. They can run the sims with a lot more processing power than we have on board. They're doing that now and will get back to me when they have something. I was hoping I wouldn't even need them, but it's not a simple fix, Blake. A direct lightning hit—"

James butted in with, "What if we can't fix this guidance system?"

Blake closed his eyes and rubbed his temple. His reply came through gritted teeth. "We require that system in order to rendezvous with our command module in lunar orbit. Without it, we'd probably miss it—it's like trying to hit a pinhead on a football field by launching a penny from the nosebleed seats. Landing on the moon was relatively easy because it was not as precise, requiring only that we land somewhere in one piece in order to survive..."

Dallas' eyes widened at this as he recalled his seat-of-the-pants landing, but he said nothing in front of Burton. Blake continued.

"But to miss the command module is certain death. We'd go shooting off into the void of deep space where we would run out of oxygen and die. Just imagine that for a moment, if you would, Mr. Burton. You and I staring at each other while our faces turn blue from lack of oxygen..."

James held Blake's eye contact for a moment and then jotted something down in his notepad.

Dallas said, "As soon as Caitlin's done, I'll see what's up with Mission Control."

#

Caitlin sat on a fixed stool in front of the communication station, talking to Ray a quarter million miles away. The quality of his transmissions was terrible, and she told him so.

"Severe dust storm about to hit Mission Control, Caitlin. We've already lost a bunch of antennae, have some broken windows...I'm not sure how much longer we'll be in communication."

Caitlin flashed on the impressive steel and glass monolithic structure that was the Spaceport America Mission Control building, and shook her head in disbelief. For some reason, she couldn't imagine those windows breaking due to a force of nature. But by some quirk of atmospherics, she heard Ray's voice come in loud and clear for the next few seconds.

"Listen: keep this between you and me, but someone's been tampering with my station computer."

Caitlin turned her head to see if she was alone, or as alone as one could possibly be in such cramped quarters. Martin and Asami were out of sight and earshot in the lab, but she could hear Blake arguing with Dallas over in the control alcove. She spoke into the transmitter. "*What*? Ray... Who would do that?"

"Caitlin, I can't discuss it in detail now, but software's been installed that tracks everything I do, logs my keystrokes. And it looks like it's being sent to—someone's coming! Gotta go. But listen: are you sure you're all right?"

"Yes, Ray, I'm fine. Don't worry about me. I'm concerned about you down there in that dust storm, and you should be, too."

"C'mon, Caitlin. Tell me the truth. Are you really okay?" Something in his tone made her shiver. Did he know something about what was going on up here? She didn't want him to think she was hiding anything from him, but she also didn't want him to worry. Not to mention Blake's orders not to spill the beans on the Negative Terrible Thing that happened up here, to jeopardize—no, to completely obliterate—Outer Limits' Perfect Safety record.

She whipped her head around again to make certain Blake wasn't paying attention. "I am okay, Ray, but Suzette is not." She went on to hurriedly explain how the marketing guru had gone missing in the tunnels and then been left behind.

"—et...isten—me..." The radio waves became static-filled again.

"You're breaking up, Ray, make it quick."

"—ver go in those tunnels again, ...me?"

"What's wrong with the tunnels? What do you know, Ray?"

He started to explain something, but it was a garbled mess, the transmission ravaged beyond all semblance of recognition. Practically, the only words she recognized in all of it were *Strat Knowles*.

And then the line of communication was severed completely.

She sat there staring at a dead radio console, thinking about Strat... He was the astronaut she had replaced. If it wasn't for him leaving, she wouldn't have her current position here. Blake had said he was a good man—a great one, even—and he was more than sorry to see him go, but that he had quit to start his own aeronautics consulting firm. High dollar stuff. He'd chosen the big bucks over the adventure, Blake had told her. The moon wasn't enough for Strat Knowles, he guessed.

Caitlin reflected on Strat. She had always wondered why an astronaut in his or her prime would leave a position that put them where an astronaut belonged—in space. She was still thinking about that when she heard Blake calling her name.

23 | ONCE MORE UNTO THE BREACH

Caitlin walked over to the control alcove, where Blake and James both stood with arms folded. Dallas occupied the console seat, but currently faced away from the controls. Caitlin could tell that Dallas had that look, the one that was as close to concern as she had ever seen him come. Just an intense sort of concentration. Blake addressed her as she walked up to them, while Dallas nodded to acknowledge her but then turned around to the console.

"We need to get back into the tunnels to look for Suzette."

Caitlin met his gaze. "I agree. But at the same time, Blake, if our oxygen supply was almost out by the time we got back here, then hers is out by now for sure."

Blake nodded. "I know that. However, there is a stash of Outer Limits equipment from earlier missions up here, including extra EVA suits and full oxygen canisters, some spare electronic parts."

"Where are those?"

"Deep in the tunnels. Deeper than we went today. But she might know how to get to them, or come across them by accident. She went deeper than we did today, that's for sure."

"If she even survived that...fall," Caitlin said, not sure how to describe what had happened to Suzette in that hellish video scene.

Blake shrugged. "As long as there's a chance—and with the additional gear, I think there is—then we have to assume she survived until we know otherwise."

James Burton nodded at this.

Dallas turned back around from the console. "I can't reach mission control. Transmission's not getting through."

Caitlin told him about her conversation with Ray, omitting mention of his suspicions in front of Blake, but telling him about the dust storm and the static-ridden connection.

Dallas nodded. "I'll try again later after doing some more work on the ship repairs. First, let me get a look at Suzette's video."

Blake handed the imaging device to him, but Burton leaned over his shoulder, intent on watching the content. Blake put a hand over the screen.

"I'm not sure you need to see this, Mr. Burton. It's intellectual property belonging to Outer Limits."

James narrowed his eyes. "The fact that I know it exists means it's going into my report, regardless. If someone higher up than me wanted to, they could demand to see it and subpoena you if necessary." Blake fumed and looked like he was about to retort but Burton kept going. "Not only that, but my personal safety is at stake up here, too, so I'd say I have a right to see it from that standpoint alone, to better understand what I've gotten myself into."

Blake reared his head back in frustration. "You're not going back to the tunnels with us, Mr. Burton. So your safety is not at stake."

"Still not true." Burton raised his pointer finger in the air. "If something happens to you two—especially her—" Burton added, taking great pleasure in emphasizing the fact that Blake himself wasn't actually needed for operating the spacecraft, "then I am in danger. I bet Dallas could fly this thing up to the Command Module on his own if he absolutely had to, but I doubt it's an optimal situation, am I right?" Burton stared directly at Dallas, who nodded matter-of-factly.

"He's right."

"I know that!" Blake's face reddened. "But we need to make an effort to find Suzette, damn it! One more trip!"

"Why can't Asami or Martin go?" James asked.

Blake shrugged. "They can go, if we can pry them out of the lab with their discovery of a lifetime, that is. But I can't go back with only them. Martin is a biologist, for Christ's sake. Of the two, Asami has more lunar experience, but she's still not an astronaut. Caitlin is specially trained on lunar EVAs, including the rovers, and that's who I want coming with me."

"Jesus, what is this?" Dallas cringed as he watched Suzette's video.

Caitlin pointed to the screen. "Looks like the floor just opened up."

"I see that. But…what's in there? It looks…"

No one had any words for him, himself included. Those who had already seen it watched the footage again to see if they could notice anything they had missed the first time around, like any sign of Suzette herself, but there was nothing of the sort.

Blake grabbed the video camera from Dallas as soon as the recording ended. "Now that we've reviewed the footage again, it's time to get underway. Caitlin, suit up, please."

She exchanged a wordless glance with Dallas before turning on a heel and heading for the airlock. But then she spun back around and directed her gaze to Blake. "What happened to Strat Knowles?"

The Outer Limits CEO, who had been looking at the video machine, looked up at Caitlin, his expression unreadable. "Strat? He left us to start his own company. Was doing quite well last I'd heard. Why—he's not working for Black Sky, is he?" He gave a lopsided grin.

"No. Seriously, Blake. What's the name of his company?"

"Why are you bringing this up now? Never mind. Tell you what." He looked at his watch. "I'll tell you the whole story on the way back to the crater, but we need to move now for Suzette's sake. Okay?"

Caitlin said nothing but nodded and this time left the alcove for good. James Burton stared at her while she walked away, while Blake watched him.

"Still not able to reach Mission Control." Dallas' back was turned to them as he worked the radio. James and Blake eyed one another behind his back. After an awkward stare-down that neither man looked away from, Blake spoke.

"Why don't you join us on the EVA, Mr. Burton? Since you weren't really uncomfortable out there after all, right?"

James shook his head. "I've already seen how the moonwalks work, and this time I want to stay in the lander to monitor the process of repairing the ship." At this, Dallas froze for a second but he said nothing and soon returned to pressing buttons on the console.

"Fine, Mr. Burton. Dallas, I'm going to the lab to see if Asami and Martin wish to accompany Caitlin and me on the EVA."

"Got it, Blake. Let me know when you're prepped for EVA so I can check you out."

Blake glared briefly at Burton before leaving for the lab.

24 | ENCOUNTERS OF THE LAST KIND

Martin adjusted the overhead lamp to better illuminate the specimen container now sitting on the small lab bench. The lab wasn't a proper laboratory; there wasn't the space, but instead was another alcove curtained off from the ship's main cabin. On the opposite side of the cramped lab, Asami worked on the only other bench, analyzing the moon rock and regolith samples she'd collected from the tunnels and crater.

Martin hunched over to stare eye level at the...*creature*, he'd taken to calling it, for lack of a better term at this point...which had burrowed into the moon dust so that only a small part of it was visible pressed up against the side. "Let me get a look at you, little guy..."

He picked up the box and upended it, forcing the creature out of the dust, where it immediately wriggled its way beneath it again. "It absolutely does not like being out of the dust," Martin concluded.

"I've got my first test results on the soil samples from the tunnels." Asami glanced at the readout of a flow injection analyzer.

"And?" Martin turned around.

"They're somewhat higher in oxygen content than the samples taken from our landing site." Both of the scientists were well-aware that although there is no oxygen in the moon's atmosphere, there is a small amount dissolved in its soil.

Martin turned back around to look at the organism, examining it closely. "I wonder if it may extract oxygen from the soil."

"How would it do that?"

"I note a series of frill-like appendages, sort of hair-like structures. Perhaps they could be something analogous to a fish's gill? A 'sand gill,' if you will?"

"Interesting..." He and Asami discussed the merits of this theory for a time, until Martin focused on the actual specimen again.

"You know, it hasn't moved for some time now." He upended the box again, which had been causing it to wriggle wildly back into the dust, but this time it remained still. Although it gave him a better view of the entire creature at once—with its bristling 'sand gills' running its entire length, and its apparently segmented body—he was concerned that it had died.

"Shock of being transported?" Asami suggested, examining a rock sample under a microscope.

"Possibly. But what I fear—if it does in fact obtain its oxygen from the soil by whatever mechanism—is that by now it's consumed all available oxygen in the cube."

Asami turned to stare at the creature as she replied. "It has been in there for some time now."

"Yes, and just as a fish in too small a bowl or tank with no air added to the water from a pump will run out of oxygen and die, I fear that could be happening with this little fellow."

"Hmmm..." Asami pointed to her bag of collected regolith. "We could add some more dust to its container and see if that revives it."

Martin nodded, still staring at the unmoving creature. He put his hand on the lid and was about to remove it when Blake and Caitlin entered the lab space.

"Hello, Martin, I'm sorry to interrupt your work." The exobiologist paused, his hand still on the box. Asami turned around from her rock samples while Blake continued.

"Caitlin and I are heading out on an EVA back to the tunnels to look for Suzette in the hope that she found the equipment stash there and may still be alive. We need for one of you two to accompany us."

Asami stood from her lab stool. "Martin should continue working with the specimen. I'll go. Not only that, but..." She paused, as if uncomfortable about voicing her thoughts.

"What?" Blake asked.

"I feel bad now about what happened with the camera during our takeoff. I was a little hard on her..."

"Don't worry, you'll have the chance to patch things up with her after we get her out of there," Blake said, before turning to Martin without skipping a beat. "I wish I could hear what you've learned so far, but for Suzette's sake we need to get going."

"Understood."

Blake and Caitlin left the lab with Asami. Martin turned back to the alien specimen.

"Now, where were we, little fellow?" He frowned as he noticed the life form was still motionless on top of its familiar dust. He slid the bag of Asami's lunar dust closer to the container so that he'd be able to have the lid off the minimal amount of time for the transfer. He thought about other ways to introduce the dust into the box without opening the lid—what if the germs from the astronauts' exhalations somehow contaminated the specimen? But short of exotic drilling tools and specialized tubing and suction equipment that he didn't have access to—not to mention time to use, since the creature could be dying—he decided the best way to proceed was a rapid manual transfer of the dust into the container via the open lid.

Martin readied a scoop of dust to pour inside. Then he removed the lid. But by the time he raised the scoop laden with lunar regolith and eyeballed the specimen again, he saw that it was swelling rapidly. In a flash he realized it: the pressurized air environment of the lunar lander was so oxygen rich compared to the animal's lunar soil environment that it had saturated it to the point that its cells were bursting.

He dropped the scoop and moved to put the lid back on the specimen box.

Too late.

The strange animal ballooned in size until its body nearly filled the entire cube, particles of dust sprinkling into the air outside the container from its swelling body. Then it burst, exploded, really, the entire organism forcefully coming apart and releasing its inner contents.

A bluish liquid splashed across Martin's face, freezing to the touch. He instinctively backed away from the creature, spitting as he felt liquid enter his mouth although it had no taste or effect that he could discern. He almost tripped but regained his balance. He stared at the sample container. The moon animal was now nothing more than a messy sludge of strange matter slopped all over the lab bench. Martin brought a latex-gloved finger to his face and it came away wet with the bluish liquid. He brushed his fingers through his hair and felt it clumping together with the sticky wetness.

He brought his hand up to his face again, over his eyes. At least he had his clear plastic safety goggles on. He went to a supply cabinet with a shatterproof plastic door and stared at his reflection. Weird, he thought. The glasses were covered in the blue stuff, but he could still see right through it even though it looked blue. And *Jesus*. That thing had exploded all over him. He looked like he'd been sprayed with silly string or some kid's art supplies.

He spotted the chemical shower hanging in a corner and ran to it.

25 | NOW YOU SEE IT, NOW YOU DON'T

"Caitlin, can you slow down?" Asami bounced around in the back of the lunar rover, descending in slow motion back to the seat with each bounce.

"Sorry, I know I'm going a little fast, but Suzette's life is at stake, Asami. I'd do the same for you, and hope you would for me, too."

Blake pointed ahead at the rover tracks they'd left earlier. "A little extra speed makes sense in this case, Asami. We'll be fine."

They approached the crater and Caitlin brought the rover to a stop on the slope, but not as high up as before. "I don't think I need to spell it out for you what would happen if our transportation gets tampered with this time," Caitlin said, exiting the vehicle. "So better to walk a little farther up the hill, because a roll from this height might not be catastrophic for our little buggy."

Blake and Asami agreed and the three of them trudged up the crater's outer slope, following their earlier tracks. They crested the rim and took a look out over the plain below, where the Black Sky lunar lander squatted in the distance. They saw no unusual activity and so continued on their way down into the crater.

On reaching the tunnel entrance, they paused and conducted a check of their suits. Satisfied the life support systems were in working order, Blake looked into the tunnel system, his headlamp illuminating the dark passage. He paid close attention to the walls and floor, but detected nothing unusual. He spoke into his helmet transmitter. "Suzette, I don't know if you can hear me, but we are coming into the tunnels after you again. If you can hear, please transmit something. Keep trying, your transmissions may be intermittent, over."

He waved an arm to Asami and Caitlin and the trio ventured into the subterranean world once again. They set out to find the ruptured wall into which Suzette had vanished. Following their earlier footprints helped to a degree, but they had to be careful not to retrace their earlier dead ends. The familiarity due to this being their second trip inside, as well as the overriding sense of purpose at rescuing Suzette, or at least locating her body, drove them forward, and they soon found themselves in the general vicinity of the spot.

Asami stared at the ground, analyzing the pattern of footprints leading off in various directions. "I could swear this was the place. " But when she looked up at the wall—at both walls, but especially on the side where she had expected the opening to be—it was solid. "This is it, isn't it? Blake?"

The Outer Limits leader stood in place while looking around. "Yes. I do think it is, but this..." He reached out and put a hand on the wall where they thought the opening had been. "This obviously isn't it, there's no opening here."

The three of them looked around in bewilderment. "We should have taken a GPS point," Asami said.

"GPS doesn't work underground." This from Caitlin.

"So we're lost." Blake slammed his fist into the wall in frustration.

Caitlin put a hand on his shoulder through the suit. "Calm down, Blake. We'll—"

And then the wall started to move.

The stone was sliding from left to right as they faced it. When Blake lifted his hand from the wall and held it frozen in midair a few inches out from the wall, they could see a reddish oval patch travel past his fingers. Slowly, though not at a glacial pace.

"Wall's moving!" Caitlin backed up a couple of steps. Asami and Blake both froze. They watched the wall begin to move faster, and then the direction of its motion changed. While continuing to move left to right, now it began to *roll* from top to bottom, as if a gigantic cylinder was being rotated as it slid along a track.

Asami pulled on Blake. "This is no rock wall! This is...this is...tell me what the hell you know about those creatures, Blake! Because that's what this is, isn't? It's a giant one of those things!"

Caitlin gasped audibly.

The billionaire backed up from the wall to where Caitlin stood. The ginormous creature continued moving, blending in with the surrounding rockscape so well that were it to be motionless it could not be detected by the casual human eye.

"I swear that I had no idea about anything like this. I mean, okay, I knew about the small creatures like the one Martin and I brought back to the lab. But I can assure you that I had absolutely no knowledge of anything like this..."

Suddenly, the lunar life form's tail end—they assumed it was the rear end since it was the last part of the body to pass by them as it moved—left a gaping hole in the rock wall. A hole exactly like the one Asami had descended into earlier.

"This is it," the selenologist declared, voice subdued with a sense of indescribable awe, wonder and dread all at once. "This is the same opening I dropped into earlier."

Caitlin leaned toward the opening to better look inside. "That means that before, this massive snake or whatever it is, just happened not to be here. That cave down there is its den, I guess. This whole tunnel complex..." Her voice faded as she looked around.

"Tell me again what happened to Strat Knowles, Blake!"

"Stop it!" Blake ordered. "Stay calm. Let's not jump to any conclusions! Martin is working as we speak on characterizing the specimen."

"I don't need anyone to characterize anything for me!" Asami trilled. "Did you see the size of that thing? We're not safe in here, Blake...and Suzette's video...what she fell into..." She peered into the hole. She lowered her voice. "Oh my God."

"What is it?" Blake also moved closer. All three of them now looked inside, the humongous animal having moved somewhere out of sight.

"The floor." Asami pointed. "It's solid again."

The three moonwalkers looked at one another through their faceplates. "Which means that one of those...*things*...is in there right now." Caitlin turned to back to stare down the hole.

Asami nodded. "These creatures—whatever they are—they are so big, and so numerous, that they actually seem to make up the tunnel walls themselves. But then when they move, empty spaces like caverns are left behind."

"The little ones are here, too," Caitlin said, lowering her head while she stared at the tunnel floor. The others turned to look and there they were: creatures the size of the one they'd collected earlier, burrowing in the lunar dirt.

"It's like this entire tunnel system is nothing but a massive den for these things," Caitlin said.

"Like we wandered into a giant insect hive," Asami agreed.

Blake ignored them, taking another step closer to the opening. "Suzette? Can you hear me? I'm here with Caitlin and Asami at the entrance to the cave you fell into earlier, over."

A few seconds passed during which the only sound was the slight rasp of their breathing in the suits.

Blake was about to say that they should go back to the LEM when they heard it.

"*—ake...I'm here... —elp me!*"

26 | ALIVE

"Suzette!" Blake shouted into his helmet transmitter while he stared into the subterranean lunar pit.

"Sounded like she said 'help me,'" Caitlin said, also peering into the void. Only Asami looked behind them and along the tunnel they were in.

"Suzette, we heard you! Where are you?"

The marketing VP's voice came again, but it was garbled and unintelligible. Sort of bubbly, like a person trying to talk underwater. They all waited a few seconds but no more transmissions came.

"I didn't get any of that," Caitlin stated.

"Me neither," Asami seconded.

"She must be too deep into that pit for the radio signals to propagate normally. Probably down into the secondary cavity." Blake turned away from the edge of the hole.

"At least we know she's alive," Caitlin said. "She must have found that equipment cache and been able to swap out her oh-two cylinder."

"And hopefully the carbon dioxide scrubber," Asami added.

Blake pointed to the climbing rope clipped to Asami's spacesuit.

"Asami, let me use your gear. I'm going in after her."

The selenologist hesitated, but only for a second.

"C'mon, Asami. Now, while there's still a chance."

"Here." She gave him the gear and prepared the rope at her end so that she could belay him as he had done for her earlier. While they set up, they continued to call out for Suzette but didn't hear her again. Then, just as Blake was about to descend into the cavernous hollow, a wrenching, haunting wail permeated their frequency.

Not words, though. Suzette, yes, but words?

"That's the weirdest sounding scream I've ever heard," Caitlin said.

"Shhhhh." Blake halted, poised with his back to the open space below them, ready to drop inside. They listened some more and heard some indecipherable sounds, very strange sounding vocalizations, unidentifiable. And then, Suzette's voice once more: "It hurts...so bad...help..." Her language degenerated into a babble of incoherent syllables.

Blake whipped his head around and eyed the pit below. The inner, deeper pit was still open. "You got me, Asami? I'm going."

"Got you." She tightened her grip on the rope and Blake rappelled down into the chamber, landing on the first level floor. He stood there a moment, this being his first trip into the hole and not exactly sure what to expect, especially with the creatures in the area. He shifted his weight from foot to foot, getting a feel for the ground, wondering if in fact it was real ground. It seemed to be.

"Looks like the pits are the spaces the creatures have left vacant, but the rest of the chamber floor is actually rock."

"Copy that," Asami returned. Communications established and as acclimated as he had time for to the new environment, Blake walked over to the end of the cavern, where the deep hole was.

He gazed down into it with trepidation, fearing that at any moment one of the life forms could come roaring up at him. But there was nothing, which was both good and bad. Good because there were no monsters lurking. But bad because, literally, he could see nothing. That black void seemed to be bottomless. He angled his head lamp this way and that, but although he could see the walls of the pit in its upper reaches, no bottom was visible.

"What's down there?" Caitlin wanted to know.

"Not a whole lot that I can see, just—"Suddenly Blake *felt* the ground tremble beneath his feet. Not quite moving, like an earthquake, but more like a series of vibrations he could feel through his booted feet, like the sub-bass at an electronic music show. "Hold on."

He looked around the room to make sure one of the creatures wasn't creeping into the space from the far end that Caitlin and Asami couldn't see. But it was all clear. He aimed his headlamp back into the pit at his feet...

...and saw rising movement. The pit was no longer pitch black as far as he could see, but now had what looked like a floor coming up at him, like an elevator. "Something's coming up!" Blake reared back as he realized whatever it was would erupt from the hole any second now.

"Move, Blake!" the two women shouted, alerting him. He was already in motion as a gigantic worm-like animal burst from the subterranean tube and shot upwards toward the opening to the main tunnel Caitlin and Asami occupied. The creature towered above him as it rocketed higher, so close that Blake could have reached out and touched it, but he did not dare. He leaned so far backwards to make sure he wouldn't be hit by the ascending snake-worm that he tripped and landed on his backside, moon-bouncing in slow motion until he stopped his motion with hands stretched out behind him. He sat there, staring up at the creature. He was about to push himself to his feet, deciding that should the animal change direction he would need to be mobile, but what he saw next rendered him absolutely motionless.

Some kind of anomaly marred the creature's side. The white-and-silver colors immediately drew Blake's eye away from the mostly grayish hues of the rest of the gargantuan body. Then he saw a splash of color and realized with a sickening, debilitating jolt of adrenaline that it was the Outer Limits logo. On a spacesuit. Suzette's spacesuit. With Suzette still in it. The space-suited form of Outer Limits' marketing executive was somehow attached to the animal. She wasn't simply holding onto the side of it, though, or merely being bounced along by the animal's motion.

Blake had to suppress the urge not to vomit in his helmet, a potentially dangerous occurrence that could have dire consequences while wearing a spacesuit. But it was difficult not to as the goliath worm-animal dragged Suzette past him and he got a close look at her.

Appendages of some sort penetrated her suit, fastening her body to the creature. But it worse than just that, Blake saw as he focused on the alien tendrils snaking *into* Suzette's body. *Through* it. The tentacle-like appendages were translucent, for he could see a liquid of some sort running through it. Altogether it had a bluish cast, but he wasn't certain if it was a clear tube structure with a blue liquid inside, or a bluish tube structure with a clear liquid inside.

How is this possible? Blake understood at this moment that Suzette hadn't found the left-behind equipment, but that the lunar dweller itself was somehow infusing her with oxygen, keeping her alive as a part of itself.

As a part of itself...

He recalled her words, just minutes ago...*It hurts...*

And then the creature bent slightly, contorted itself enough to be able to fit through the opening through which Blake had come down here, and he was suddenly helmet-to-helmet with Suzette Calderon. In the most surreal moment of his entire life, Blake Garner made eye contact with his employee.

"Suzette!"

He saw her part her lips to speak, but by then the creature's head—if it was a head—had emerged into the tunnel where the screams of Caitlin and Asami drowned out all other sound on the comm channel. He reached out a hand to grab onto Suzette—saw that hers were pinned tightly behind her back, while her legs were immobilized—her feet actually disappearing into the creature's flesh itself. A tube the diameter of a garden hose ran up through her chin into her mouth, disappearing to where, Blake could only imagine.

His hand slid off her spacesuit and she was carried higher by the alien beast. Blake watched helplessly as the animal passed through the fractured wall. It turned left, heading deeper into the tunnel system with Suzette in tow, her bubbly, distorted grunts echoing in their headsets.

27 | IF IT ISN'T ONE THING

Blake stared up out of the chamber until he saw the creature's tail end pass through into the tunnel. He heard Caitlin 's voice.

"Blake, get out of there! Hurry, before it comes back."

"C'mon Blake!" Asami added.

He felt the slack in his rope tighten as Asami prepared to belay him up. But now that the creature had left, he couldn't resist taking a good look down into the deep chasm from which it had come. He turned around and directed his headlamp back into the pit. In it he saw a vision of Hell, a vacant hole seething with moving flesh, the floor opening and closing as giant worms passed through. Or snakes. Whatever the hell they were. But he knew one thing: he had been absolutely right that they had mistaken the very walls and floors and ceilings of this tunnel network for rock, when much of it was living flesh, constantly changing the configuration of the network of passages as they moved about. The humans were inside their hive, in an alien catacomb of sorts, assuming that if the creatures lived here, they must also die here. The notion made him nauseous and he turned away as Asami yelled at him again.

"Now, Blake!"

He moved to the wall below the opening, where he looked up to see Asami staring down at him, a glint of light from his headlamp reflecting off of her faceplate. He couldn't see Caitlin but knew she'd be facing out into the tunnel, watching for more creatures. He "walked" up the wall, a task made easier in the low gravity—which he was grateful to discover was an actual rock wall and not some sort of living thing—while Asami pulled him up with the rope. He got a look at Asami's eyes when he stepped back into the main tunnel; she was visibly shaken at having seen Suzette pass by her, raked across the wall by the worm-creature. She and Suzette had not gotten along well, but she would never wish this kind of fate on anybody. The spaceship incident with the camera seemed so trivial now.

"Thanks," he said to Asami, unclipping his rope harness. "It went that way, right?" He pointed to their left, the direction that led deeper into the tunnel system.

"Yes." Caitlin's voice sounded weak. She, too, had been traumatized by what she had witnessed.

Blake checked his oxygen gauge. "We could chase after it for a little while, see if we might be able to rescue Suzette when it stops—rip her out of it—"

"No!"

"Blake!" Caitlin was even more forceful than Asami. It surprised her that he would put himself on the line for Suzette to that degree. It wasn't heroism, though, that was the troubling thing. She knew it was the desire to save his own company's reputation from the fallout that would surely result from a death—and a spectacularly hideous death at that. He wanted to save her only because it would save Outer Limits in the process. "There's no way we can save her. Did you see her? It's like she was a part of that thing…like…"

"Like it had injected her with its own blood vessels or something like that?"

Caitlin nodded, the reflection of Blake's headlamp bobbing crazily in her faceplate.

"We need to worry about ourselves, Blake," Asami cut in. "I can't end up like that…I—"

She choked off a sob, envisioning herself entombed like Suzette into the one of the organisms, being dragged through the series of lunar burrows, for what purpose, she had no idea, but she couldn't imagine a more horrible fate.

And it hurts. *Help… it hurts!*

Suzette's plea echoed in her brain until she could take it no more and she turned to leave in the opposite direction the creature went.

"Okay," Blake relented. "We'll leave."

"Good." Caitlin breathed a sigh of relief as she turned to follow Asami toward the exit. She had been concerned that Blake's judgment might be clouded by knowing that this horrendous event marked the end of his dreams of space leadership that he might do something stupid. But he fell into line after Caitlin and Asami, head on a swivel as he looked around for signs of the creatures while they progressed toward the exit.

They moved fast, bounding through the twisty passages, using their footprints to guide them, avoiding contact with the walls. A couple of small creatures wriggled here and there on the floor, but by the time they emerged out onto the crater's inner slope, they had seen none of the larger ones. Asami hypothesized that perhaps the bigger individuals needed to stay deeper in the soil, that the larger they got, the deeper they ventured. She noted slightly higher oxygen readings in the soil samples taken from deeper underground.

"Can't say as I give a crap about it right now, Asami," Caitlin said. "I just want to get back to the LEM in one piece."

"I won't argue with that," Asami said.

Blake led the way up the crater slope. As soon as they topped over the rim, they heard Dallas' voice on the comm channel.

"Dallas to Outer Limits EVA party, do you copy, over?" he repeated himself.

Blake replied. "We copy you, Dallas. We just came out of the tunnels, now on the crater rim, over."

He paused to look out over the plains while he waited for Dallas to respond. That their rover was still there was the first thing he confirmed. And in the distance: a gleam of light off of Black Sky's LEM. But he saw no EVA activity between that ship and the rover, no space-suited figures slinking away after having sabotaged their ride.

"Suzette?"

"We couldn't save her."

"She wasn't down in the pit?"

Blake flashed on the hideous monstrosity of the worm with Suzette infused into its physiology. He shuddered while he spoke. "Dallas, I'll fill you in on the details when we get back to the LEM."

"She's not dead," Caitlin blurted.

"What?" Dallas sounded uncharacteristically stunned.

Blake reached out and swatted Caitlin on the shoulder, glaring at her through their helmets. That didn't shut her up, though.

"She's...it's so awful Dallas...we *saw* her, and she's alive, technically, but..."

"She's *alive*? Why didn't you bring her back? Blake, what's going on?"

Blake's voice rose in pitch along with his anger. "I told you, Dallas, I'll fill you in on the details when we get back. Suffice it to say for now that we could not rescue her. Now tell me about the status of the ship repairs, *over*."

A lengthy pause ensued while Dallas digested this heavy development. Blake wondered if James Burton had overheard the radio message. "I concluded my troubleshooting of the guidance system, Blake, and I'm afraid the news is not good." After a chorus of exasperated sighs, Dallas continued. "There's an electronic part I need in order to fix it, and we do not carry a spare."

Blake threw his head back in aggravation before responding. "Copy that, Dallas. Did you try contacting Mission Control to ask them to advise as to what, if any, components might be cannibalized out of other, less essential systems so that you might build the part we need?"

Caitlin nodded silently. It was a good idea, worth a try, since Mission Control had the man- and computer-power to comb through all of the ship's specifications quickly, looking for a match with whatever resources were known to be aboard the spaceship. They could then instruct the astronauts accordingly. The approach had worked famously well on the ill-fated yet non-catastrophic Apollo 13 lunar mission.

But again, Dallas had bad news. "I tried, Blake, but was unable to establish communication, probably due to the dust storm at the spaceport they mentioned was approaching the last time I did talk to them."

Silently, Caitlin corroborated this, but she didn't want to bring up that she'd spoken to Ray, since he told her about Strat Knowles.

"But I've got another idea," Dallas came back before Blake could voice his displeasure.

"Go ahead."

They heard Dallas clear his throat. "Bear with me here, Blake. You might not like this on the surface, but I've thought it through and am convinced it's our best shot at getting this system fixed in time."

The phrase *in time* was an unspoken threat none of them needed to be reminded of, meaning that if they couldn't fix the lander's guidance system before their oxygen supply ran out, they'd have no choice but to attempt to rendezvous with the orbiting Command Module without it, a near-impossible task that almost surely would have them careening out into the void of space forever entombed in the LEM.

"Go ahead, Dallas."

"You have a visual on Black Sky's lander, correct?"

Blake glanced across the plain at his competitor's LEM. "That's affirmative."

"You could drive over there and ask them for the part we need—an actuator—and then bring it back to me."

A non-verbal passage of air issued from Blake's mouth that made it clear he was not at all comfortable with this idea. They all knew that to have to approach Kennedy Haig, Blake's longtime business rival, would be less than palatable for him.

"I know you don't like asking for help, Blake," Dallas said, "from anybody much less Kennedy, but we're really in a bind here."

"They sabotaged our rover!" Blake returned. "What makes you so sure they'd want to help us? Seems like quite the opposite to me."

Caitlin voiced her opinion. "Blake, listen. Dallas is right. Obtaining that part is the easiest way to solve our problem. If Black Sky has one they're willing to give us—and if they do, I bet they will— then that's the simplest solution. Otherwise, what? At best, we wait some indeterminate period of time before communications with Mission Control are reestablished, and then explain the problem to them and wait for them to get back with a solution—assuming they can come up with one—and then we have to execute on it..."

She and Asami stared at him while Dallas reiterated that Black Sky was absolutely worth a try. "Please, for our sake, just put the bad blood between you and Kennedy aside for now in order to act like professionals and save our lives!" Caitlin pleaded.

Blake threw up his hands. "All right. Fine. We'll go visit Black Sky. They'll probably think we're there about our rover, but then when I ask about the part instead, it'll throw Kennedy for a loop, and I'll enjoy that."

The three of them started toward the rover until Dallas spoke again. "There's one more thing I should tell you. About the creatures."

"Go ahead." Blake was pretty sure that he already knew all he wanted to know about those creatures. He resumed walking toward the rover, waving for the others to follow him.

"Martin had an incident with the specimen in the lab."

"What happened?" Blake was becoming inured to bad news. It just kept coming, and he knew they couldn't really handle much more, but at the same time he just didn't seem to care. Whatever it was, he would deal with it. He had no choice.

"Martin says that the creatures—he says they may actually be worms although he's not yet certain because he didn't get a chance to dissect it—"

"Why didn't he get a chance to dissect it? He didn't want to kill it, I guess, since it's the only one? Well, you can tell him not to worry about that; there are plenty more where that one came from." Uncomfortable laughter from Caitlin and Asami.

"No, that's not it. It exploded before he had the chance."

"Exploded?"

"Yeah, as soon as he took the lid off the specimen container. Nothing left of it except liquid that sprayed all over his face."

"*What*?!"

"Sounds like you heard me correctly."

Blake reached the rover but he stood there without getting in while he concentrated on the radio exchange. "Is he okay?"

"No, he's sick now."

"He's not praying yet, is he? Because if an atheist starts to pray, you know he's sick as a dog, am I right?"

No one laughed. "It's really not funny, Blake. He doesn't look good at all, and seems to be getting worse. In fact, I have to get back to him now to evaluate possible surgical options, which is another reason to obtain this part from Black Sky—one less thing for me to deal with."

"I'll let you get back to it then," Blake said, the closest he was likely to come to an apology.

"Real quick, let me tell you what Martin did find out before this happened. He said that these life forms will be attracted to high concentrations of oxygen, since oxygen is a limiting factor in their environment and they apparently have evolved to extract minute quantities of it from the soil."

Asami nodded. "Makes sense, since all of the ones we've found so far have been underground."

"Carry on." Blake climbed behind the wheel of the rover while Caitlin took the shotgun seat and Asami got in the back. He pointed the vehicle toward the Black Sky lunar lander and accelerated.

28 | IS ANYBODY IN THERE?

Blake had the rover at maximum speed, jostling them around as they approached their rival's LEM. About the same size as theirs, a squat, polygonal thing with highly reflective surfaces, it was the lone human-made structure in sight, with the exception of the rover itself. When they were close enough that he worried they might think they were trying to ram them in retaliation for destroying their other rover, he cut speed, coasting to a stop a few meters from the craft.

The trio of moon explorers sat in the rover, watching the spaceship.

"I don't see any lights on at all," Caitlin pointed out.

"No signs of activity whatsoever, really," Asami added.

"Should we walk up and knock?" Caitlin asked without moving from the rover.

Blake fiddled with controls on his spacesuit. "Let me try to raise them on the radio first. I'd prefer not to surprise them too much by knocking on the door." Blake tried various radio frequencies to get in touch with Black Sky, including Mission Control, but received no response.

"Mission Control is still down?" Caitlin's voice belied her concern.

Blake nodded. "Looks that way."

"What should we do?" Asami glanced around at the ground surrounding the rover. Saw nothing unusual. Blake flashed the rover's headlights at the LEM. Waited a few seconds and did it again. Still no reaction. He dismounted from the rover. Caitlin and Asami followed suit.

They walked up to the lander's entry hatch and observed it. No discernible activity. They tried knocking on the side of the craft. Again, no response.

As they turned around to go back to the rover, they saw two moonwalkers wearing different suits from those of Outer Limits approaching over a small rise. Blake suggested they walk toward them to greet them, so they don't feel threatened that they might be sabotaging their ship. When they had walked for only a few seconds their shared comm channel crackled with a new voice.

"This is Black Sky EVA party to Outer Limits, do you copy?"

Blake didn't hesitate to respond. "We copy you, Black Sky."

"State your intentions, over."

"Don't worry, we come in peace. Right, girls?"

Blake knew the two professional women would be miffed at being referred to as 'girls', but he had to do something to seem amenable to Black Sky. Perhaps they wouldn't feel as threatened knowing that two out of three of the visitors were female?

The pair of moonwalkers slowed their steps as they neared the newcomers. "What is it that you want?"

Blake didn't recognize the voice. He was glad that it wasn't his old enemy, Kennedy Haig. He'd have to see him inside the ship, of that he was sure, but somehow not having to see him right now made him feel much better. "We have a favor to ask of you. We need a part for our guidance system and were hoping you might be able to assist us."

"I didn't know we were in the lunar hardware business," one of the Black Sky men joked to the other, eliciting a hearty laugh. "But seriously, we'd have to clear that type of request with Kennedy. He's inside, taking a nap, probably."

"Can we come in?" Blake asked.

The two spacewalkers stepped up to the Outer Limits rivals and stared at them, helmet to helmet. Caitlin noticed that their suits were extremely dusty, almost as if they'd been rolling around on the ground.

Suddenly, a new voice broke in over the comm. "Blake, old chum. Caught me in my afternoon nap. No matter where we are, you still always find a way to borrow something from me, don't you? Money...ideas...spare spacecraft parts...."

An uncomfortable silence ensued that was broken by Kennedy himself. "It's okay, let them in. Go ahead. They're welcome for a few minutes, at least."

The two Black Sky astronauts turned in the direction of their lander. "This way." They walked toward it with the Outer Limits team close behind. Caitlin's gaze wandered a few feet off to her left and she saw movement. Then she realized it was a slew of the small creatures, rolling, digging, writhing in the lunar soil. She picked up her pace, catching up to the others. She saw no reason to bring it up right now.

Then the lander's airlock door was opening and the two Black Sky astronauts welcomed the Outer Limits team inside.

29 | IN THE BELLY OF THE BEAST

"You can take your helmets off now. We're pressurized." The two Black Sky astronauts who'd escorted the Outer Limits team inside waved toward the main cabin of the lander, where three other spacemen, none of whom wore a spacesuit, waved in awkward greeting. Caitlin removed her helmet first, then Asami, and then, as though shy to reveal his face, Blake. When everyone inside had removed their helmets, they said nothing for a few seconds while they looked at one another, especially Blake and Kennedy. Moon dwellers, all, united by a common bond of deep space travel.

"Greetings, Earthlings, I am Kennedy Haig!" Everyone laughed except Blake, but even he cracked a smile.

"I bet you always wanted to say that!" Caitlin said, eager to break the ice.

"You know it. And who might you lovely ladies be?"

At this, Blake cocked his head to one side. "Seriously, Kennedy. You know who they are. Like you haven't studied our crew roster."

Caitlin shot Blake a cautioning glance that said, *Ease up, we're here to ask this guy for a big favor!*

But Kennedy didn't seem to take offense. A man of medium height and build with short brown, curly hair, he shrugged it off. "Yes, well, a lot's been on my mind lately." He looked about his ship, and the others followed his gaze. Now that Blake took a closer look, things didn't seem all that perfect, certainly not what the world had come to expect from shooting star Kennedy Haig. Much of the cabin was cast in darkness, the air was uncomfortably warm, and a small cascade of liquid splattered on the floor in a corner.

Before Blake could ask about the condition of the ship, Kennedy indicated the man to his left. He introduced him as Pete

Stenson. "This gentleman, you should know, is our FAA representative."

At this, Blake nodded cordially. "Ah yes, we came down with a case of one of those as well. We left him back at the ship." But the shared joke between them didn't last. "So tell me, Kennedy," Blake asked point blank, or *Point Blake,* as a leading business magazine had once headlined its cover with, featuring a photo of the Space 2.0 entrepreneur beneath. "What's going on here?"

Kennedy swiveled his head this way and that, as if having trouble finding something in disarray. "Going on? What...oh, the general state of disarray, is that what you mean?"

"That's precisely what I mean."

Kennedy gave a noncommittal gesture. "Living on the moon isn't easy, old chum. But I guess you knew that, since here you are to beg for spare parts, I'm told, is that it?"

"Easy, Kennedy, they're just—" one of the Black Sky astronauts began, before Kennedy cut him off.

"Hold on, Arnie, okay? Let me check for the part. I'll be right back." Kennedy turned and walked into an alcove toward the rear of the ship, followed by another of his crew. The other two—Arnie ("Arnold Strausen, but call me Arnie") and an Asian man who introduced himself as Takeo Matsuda—along with Pete Stenson, the Black Sky flight FAA rep, walked closer to the Outer Limits group until Stenson spoke to them in a low voice.

"There's no time to waste so I'll get right to the point. It's my professional assessment that Kennedy's pride is keeping him from admitting how bad things really are here."

One of the Black Sky astronauts chimed in. "The condition of the ship is even worse than it looks."

Stenson went on after nodding. "It's true. This ship is not in operational condition. We could not leave the moon right now if we wanted to."

"What about our rover? What happened to it?" Caitlin asked.

Takeo nodded while casting an unwavering glance her way. "I admit that we did that— Arnie, here," he said, indicating the astronaut standing next to him, who frowned along with an unenthusiastic wave, "and myself. But I can assure you that the serious damage was a complete accident. We only intended to scavenge non-essential electrical parts from it that were not critical to its functioning, but I accidently tripped and grabbed onto it to break my fall, which unfortunately sent it tumbling down the crater."

"We're very sorry," Arnie finished, while Caitlin gave an *a-ha* nod. The mystery of the lunar rover had been solved.

Blake glanced toward the back of the ship, where Kennedy was not yet visible. "Did the rover parts enable you to make your repairs, or will they?"

Stenson and the two Black Sky spacemen shook their heads in unison. "They did not. One of the capacitors we took turned out to be the wrong size. We're stuck here until we can fix this ship, and right now we're stymied as to how to do it. Is that a correct assessment, gentlemen?" He deferred to the two astronauts, both of whom nodded emphatically.

"What caused the technical problems with the ship in the first place?" Caitlin asked.

Stenson cast a backward glance before responding. "Basically I'd say it's engineering failures precipitated by Kennedy Haig pushing the timetable too hard to get into space, to beat your team. Pure and simple," he concluded with a shrug. No one disagreed, but no one agreed either, so Stenson pressed his case, clearly scared for his own safety at this point.

"It's my contention that Kennedy deliberately withheld information about the state of certain spacecraft systems from the FAA and other regulatory agencies in the days prior to launch, information that had it been known would have led to a Black Sky launch delay."

"Excuse me? What nonsense did I just hear?" They jumped at the voice of Kennedy, who had appeared in the center of the ship without being heard, still some distance away but probably close enough to follow the conversation.

"Relax, Kennedy," Blake said, "we were just discussing the ships, yours and mine, and trying to figure out what needs to be done so that we can both get back to one hundred percent working order again."

"That's not what it sounded like to me," Kennedy said, eyeing Stenson. "It sounded to me like Mr. Stenson, here, was accusing me of negligence!" He stepped to within arm's reach of the FAA man. "Is there something you'd like to say to my face?"

Stenson stood his ground. "No. You can read about it in the report I submit. If we can manage to get back home, that is."

"What do you intend to report?" Kennedy's gaze bored into Stenson's eyes.

"I intend to report exactly what I observed happening here, which is that in your rush to be first to the moon and beat your competitor here," Stenson said, nodding to Blake, "you took shortcuts that compromised—"

Kennedy shoved Stenson back with a hand on his shoulder. "Bullshit!"

Blake and Arnie separated to the two men, Blake standing in front of Stenson and the Black Sky man in front of Kennedy.

"Hold it, hold up, everybody!" Blake shouted. They all eyed him expectantly, including Kennedy.

"I have a solution that should enable us to fix both of our ships."

30 | TEAMWORK

Once he had everyone's attention, Blake spoke. "There is a small cache of Outer Limits equipment inside a network of underground tunnels in the nearby crater." He paused to see if mention of the tunnels triggered any recognition, but everyone from Black Sky appeared genuinely stunned.

"Tunnels, you say?" Kennedy asked, his curiosity overcoming his recent adrenaline surge.

Asami nodded, figuring that this was her opportunity to showcase her expertise and reason for being on the moon in the first place. "That's right. There's an extensive tunnel system beneath the crater's interior that, from what little preliminary investigating and firsthand observations I've been able to do so far, appear to have been formed..." Her mouth tugged down at the corners as she broke herself off.

"Formed how?" Kennedy prodded. "What's the matter?"

Asami looked confused. "I'm a selenologist. I came here to study the moon's geological processes and learn more about how it formed. When I first saw the tunnel system—the first time I even heard about it was after I arrived on the moon on this trip—" she said, narrowing her eyes ever so briefly at Blake, "I thought it must be similar to a lava tube. But now..." Again she trailed off, unsure of how to broach the subject of the creatures and how the tunnels may in fact be the result of biological, rather than geological, activity.

Caitlin picked up on this and made eye contact with Blake, prompting him to address it, but it was Kennedy who broke into the pause.

"So you mean to tell me that there are *tunnels* beneath McMurdo crater right over there?"

All of the Outer Limits people nodded. Kennedy remained silent, contemplating this.

"That is correct," Blake said. He glanced over at Caitlin again before continuing. "But listen. We have gear in that stockpile that can help both of us. I'm more than willing to share it." He eyed Kennedy directly with this last statement. "However, there are risks to obtaining it far beyond those associated with a normal EVA."

A round of quizzical looks from the Black Sky team ensued, and Blake went on. "We have oxygen canisters there, some raw electrical components that can be utilized for any number of purposes, and even extra spacesuits. But to get to it we need to brave certain biological hazards."

"Please explain," Kennedy said, eyes alight with curiosity.

All eyes were on Blake as they waited for him to speak. "There are living animals of some kind underground. Like worms or snakes. Some of them are very large." He paused to let that sink in. Arnie and Takeo exchanged knowing glances and then Kennedy spoke up.

"We've seen small ones around the ship—right outside. We weren't sure what to make of them at first, but..."

Caitlin nodded slowly, recalling what she'd seen on the way into the Black Sky lander. Kennedy continued.

"At first, we thought we were suffering some kind of space-induced psychosis—agoraphobia or something, but we all kept seeing them."

"They seem to have increased in number the last day or so, though," one of Kennedy's crew said, eliciting nods from the others.

"They seem harmless enough," Kennedy ventured. All three Outer Limits personnel shook their heads wordlessly until Blake said, "They're not harmless." Then he recounted what happened to Suzette as horror registered in the eyes of their hosts. Blake completed his account, and then, when Asami started to provide more detail at the urging of a Black Sky astronaut, Kennedy waved her down.

"I've heard enough, thank you. I get it. But I don't think we have much choice here, do we?" he asked, looking at his crew in turn. "They've got gear we can use. We need to help them get it."

Blake nodded. "We couldn't carry it all with just the three of us, and multiple trips are not an option, it's too far."

"Then we go. Myself and one volunteer," he said, looking at his crew. "Not you, Mr. Stenson." The FAA man said nothing, most likely glad he did not have to go on the risky outing.

Takeo said he would go while Arnie and another astronaut—a quiet but observant man introduced as Jack Williams— stayed behind to continue work on repairing the ship.

Without delay, the EVA party of five—three Outer Limits and Two Black Sky—donned their spacesuits and entered the airlock. "Good luck," they heard from Arnie just before they stepped outside. They weren't prepared for what they saw.

The ground teemed with small creatures, writhing and wriggling and squirming across the top layers of moon dust. The soil seemed positively alive with them, like a school of fish at the surface of the ocean. Not only that, but their presence didn't seem to be localized around the LEM; a long line of the life forms stretched all the way to the crater.

"So many of them now!" Takeo said.

"We haven't seen this many in one place before," Blake admitted before adding nervously, "but at least these are the small ones."

Caitlin studied the side of the lander. A dense conglomeration of burrowing creatures festered along one side of the LEM. She turned to face Kennedy. "Do you have an external oxygen leak? Our exobiologist said they could be evolved to extract oh-two from the soil—and this is just my own personal guess—but pure oxygen is something they'd normally never be exposed to on the moon, so if it's leaking from your ship, maybe we're finding out now that they're attracted to it."

Kennedy looked back to his LEM and followed the trail of animals with his eyes. "So they could actually be drawn to it from some distance away?"

Caitlin nodded. "Like ants to a pile of sugar."

"Or like sharks to blood in the water," Asami said.

The group stood there silently for a few moments, watching the alien activity on the ground until Blake started walking the rest of the way to the rover. "We best get going."

"Nice toy, Blake," Kennedy said when they got to the vehicle.

"This toy—the remaining one after your people got done trying to cannibalize the other one, I might add—"

"Blake," Caitlin warned softly.

"—is going to get us to the crater quickly, and back here with our stash of equipment."

"We're all going to fit?" Takeo asked.

Blake shrugged. "It's made for four people, and we're a crew of five on this little sortie, but I think it'll hold us, don't you think, Caitlin?"

The astronaut nodded. "It should. Would be better if we still had two, though, especially since we'll hopefully be returning with equipment," she couldn't help but adding.

"I apologize for that,'" Kennedy said. "But can we just move forward, please? There's nothing else I can do about it now except to cooperate with you to fix our ships."

They boarded the rover. Blake took the wheel with Caitlin riding up front. Asami squeezed into the back with the two Black Sky men, Takeo hanging a little over the side. They made the drive to the crater, noticing that the stream of creatures was unbroken the entire way, like a moving river of living animals from crater to the LEM. Kennedy made radio contact with his astronauts in the lander to warn them they should get that oxygen leak shut off ASAP, that it was attracting the creatures.

When they arrived at the crater, Blake parked only a little ways up from the base and the five of them exited the moon buggy. They had to skirt around the line of smallish animals making their way down from the crater. In some spots, they could only see the ground itself moving, puffs of dust being thrown out, but in others they saw the actual bodies of the aliens, lined with the frilled "sand gills" Martin had discovered. They could also see that a few of them were larger than the others.

The expedition made its way up the outer crater slope. "First time up here?" Blake asked Kennedy.

"No, we did climb up here once to have a look down inside, but we never ventured down in there. I see you're a little more used to the hop you need to move efficiently up the side."

Blake laughed as he bunny-hopped toward the rim of the crater. "Practice makes perfect."

A throng of creatures poured and tumbled over the rim. They gave them a wide berth as they stepped over and down into the crater's interior. Blake led the way down into the crater, explaining that the rock outcroppings that dotted the slope were actually tunnel entrances. They could see that the creatures poured in thin lines from several of the higher openings, but not from the ones deeper inside the crater, as if they knew they needed to leave the crater higher up by the rim.

The team had to step over a line of the worms a couple of times, but they managed to reach the same tunnel entrance Outer Limits had been using without incident. Caitlin was surprised, however, when Blake passed this and continued to descend deeper into the crater.

"Where are we going?" she asked, which caused concern among the Black Sky team.

"I thought all of you have been inside the tunnels before?" Kennedy asked.

"It's a different tunnel that leads to the equipment cache, and only I have been to that one before," Blake explained.

They made their way further into the crater, stopping about three tunnel entrances lower than the one Outer Limits had used earlier. They all activated their helmet lights and peered inside. To Caitlin and Asami, it didn't look much different than the other one.

Blake made a final check of his suit and gauges, and then led the way into the tunnel.

31 | AFTERLIFE

"Be right there, Martin." Dallas finished putting on his anti-biocontamination gear—face shield, rubber gloves, scrubs, the works. It was time to do what he could for Martin, whose condition had deteriorated significantly in the last hour. James watched Dallas adjust his face mask for the fourth time.

"He's really sick, isn't he?"

"Yes."

"He's going to die, isn't he?"

"I don't know, James. I'm going to evaluate him and see what I can do to help."

It was not lost on Dallas that James did not volunteer to go with him into the lab where Martin was, either to help in some way or to do his job as an observer of shipboard practices. Dallas' mind echoed the thought that he knew bounced around in James' brain. *What if whatever Martin got from that thing is contagious?*

The exobiologist was lying down on a cot Dallas had set up for him in the lab. Dallas, an experienced former trauma surgeon, sucked in his breath at the sight of his patient. Martin's skin was entirely a bluish, purplish color. The color of venous blood. And yet his skin was oddly translucent, but with a bluish cast. It sort of reminded him of the realistic anatomical models he had studied with in medical school, in addition to human cadavers. And worse, his veins. *Veins*, Dallas emphasized to himself. For he couldn't see any arteries. Even though his skin—all of it that he could see, anyway—his arms, hands, face, neck...was weirdly clear. Yet there were no *arteries*—that was it, Dallas realized. No arteries, only veins. All of his blood vessels were blue, or perhaps purplish—the same hue as the rest of his skin, where he supposed that his blood vessels and capillaries had burst, releasing their micro-rivers of blood to flood the body cavities.

He knew that blood was actually red, from hemoglobin, even though in veins it appeared blue through normal skin because it lacked oxygen, since veins carried blood back to the heart after their blood had been depleted of oxygen during its travels throughout the body. Then that same blood, after being pumped out of the heart, would be full of fresh oxygen again to tour the body anew via the arterial system. But Martin's blood vessels were all the same color—as if all he had were veins, *or as if all of his blood was devoid of oxygen.*

He was so stunned by the implications that it took him a bit to realize Martin was talking. Ranting, really, in rapid, monotonic bursts about how ironic it was that the first interaction of human-alien life resulted in the death of not only likely himself, but also the creature. He ended with a, "What do you think, doc?" which caught Dallas by surprise.

He cleared his throat and said, "It's only a weak hypothesis at this point, but it's possible that when the creature's blood entered your system, its specialized oxygen-gathering cells—if it has cells— went into overdrive in our spacecraft's relatively oxygen-rich environment, causing your blood vessels to rupture, basically to have a massive, circulatory system-wide aneurism."

Martin's expression changed then, at the realization that he was in critical condition, on the moon, so very far from help, if he even could be helped. He knew that Dallas was his only hope if there was hope at all.

"Let me hook you up to an IV," the physician said, wheeling one next to the cot. He prepped Martin's arm, noticing how easily it bruised with the ordinary contact needed to swipe it with an alcohol pad, and then further with the needle injection. Dallas then went about setting up machines to monitor Martin's vital signs, the results of which were highly discouraging. Dallas was stone-faced as he looked at the readouts while Martin's face grew paler under the lab lights.

"I'm not going to sugarcoat this for you, Martin. There's no time for that. Short of a major blood transfusion operation, which we are not equipped for here, I'm not sure if there is anything I can do to save you."

"I—" Martin began but then broke off, one of contemporary society's most eloquent writers and speakers on philosophical matters at a loss for words.

"Save your energy." At this, Martin seemed to relax.

"You are bleeding internally, Martin. Very severely, because your blood vessels have all ruptured. That's why all of your skin has turned blue."

"Am I...am I contagious? The creature gave me this condition?"

"I don't think so. I think it's more of an oxygen-related phenomenon where your cells are splitting—lysis, it's called—with the introduction of whatever mechanisms are present in the moon animal's fluids that you came into contact with."

Suddenly, Martin was racked with spasms. Dallas held him down while continuing to talk to him. He raised his voice to be heard above the rattling cot. "Martin, listen to me. You don't have to say anything. Just listen."

The stricken biologist continued to jerk and twist but his eyes seemed to regain some measure of light as he held Dallas' gaze.

"I don't think you have much time left, Martin." He found he had to concentrate on not saying the words, "on this Earth," since they were on the moon. In his hospital days, he had seen ministers deliver many a bedside prayer to patients, and while he was no priest, he was familiar enough with the language that he could approximate it if it would offer comfort to the patient. He could do nothing else, after all.

"If you like, I can say a prayer for you. No one has to know about it," he added, in a nod to Martin's outspoken atheism. He knew the man publicly did not believe in God, but when someone was about to go, he thought it was best to give them the option. Besides, he knew that Martin's atheism was big business for him; he'd made a celebrity career out of it, after all, so what if it was only an act?

But Martin's next words dispelled that notion. "Say a prayer for yourself if it makes you feel any better, Dallas. You're going to need all the help you can get."

And with that, a gush of dark purple blood oozed from Martin's mouth, the monitoring machines began frantically beeping, and he flat-lined.

32 | ASKING FOR DIRECTIONS

The tunnels all looked the same. They'd been walking, searching for a landmark, anything to let them know that they'd made some progress. But the gray passageways were indecipherable in their sameness. They saw no footprints, but making matters worse was the fact that the ground here was hard rock with a very thin to non-existent dust layer, too thin to leave footprints. For the Black Sky members of the party, it was all a new experience and they simply took it in, marveling at the subterranean world so close to their spacecraft. But for Outer Limits, and Caitlin in particular, the wandering carried ramifications.

"Blake, haven't we been past this junction before?"

"Don't think so. I think it's just up ahead here."

"You keep saying that, and we keep circling around!"

"This is definitely the same passage we came through before," Asami said, running a gloved hand along a distinct pattern of striations along a tunnel wall. "Look at this, how unusual it is. I remember it."

Blake slammed a booted foot into the regolith and turned to look at the wall. "Forgive me for not knowing the entire goddamned moon inside and out like the back of my hand. I'm doing the best I can." He said nothing further and plodded off down the tunnel.

"I don't think I need to remind you," Caitlin said, "that this is a situation where your best might not be good enough. It's not about effort here, Blake. It's about right or wrong. Period. You're right: we live. You're wrong: we die. Which is it?"

Suddenly, Blake spun and faced Caitlin as she nearly bumped into him while she walked along. "Was it about *right or wrong*, Caitlin, when you and Dallas landed the LEM far enough off course that finding our planned destinations became an issue in the first place?"

Silence, as the group huddled in the tunnel.

"Or was that effort?"

Still nothing.

"Because if I'm not mistaken, that wasn't really good enough, now was it?"

"Past mistakes shouldn't lower the bar, should they Blake?" Kennedy's voice reminded them all that there was a complex dynamic here. This was no longer Outer Limits' problem alone.

They all heard Blake take a deep breath. "If you would all just allow me to concentrate on my path, I'm confident that I can find what we're looking for."

"Blake, I will say this for you," Kennedy said. "Back during our first startup—that early web transaction thing—you always had a knack for getting people to keep forging ahead, even when there was no clear path. *Especially* when there was no clear path, I think. You kept us all moving, when it meant death to stand still. The only thing, though, Blake? You weren't always right, either. Sometimes you were. I just hope this is one of those times, Mr. Garner. Carry on."

They did just that, creeping through the eerie system of underground passages, periodically checking their suit systems to catch a malfunction as early as possible, to monitor the supply of oxygen keeping them alive in this hostile environment. Blake stayed at the front of the pack and a couple of times, after they turned down a tunnel, he would suddenly step back around, hand outstretched, telling them to turn back because he'd led them down what he could see was a dead end. But after a while, Caitlin and Asami agreed they were definitely in new territory. They encountered no footprints on these new paths.

Still wary of every ceiling and floor lest they be alive, the group forged on. The grumblings about whether Blake would be able to find his stash location were starting up again when they passed into an open cave. A pile of equipment sat in the middle of it, so foreign in this otherwise completely natural environment. A spacesuit stained with bluish brown splotches minus a body lay nearby. The spacewalkers piled into each other as those first into the cavern stopped in their tracks to take in the unusual scene.

"Is that blood on that suit... Is that Suzette?" Caitlin managed after some time.

"It looks like it could be deoxygenated blood," Asami observed.

Blake took a couple of tentative steps toward the blood-caked mess. "First of all, there's no one in that suit. It's just a suit. Second of all, it's missing the helmet, which could mean that whoever was using it somehow switched suits after incurring damage..."

"It says KNOWLES," Caitlin said, glaring at Blake through their faceplates. No one said anything until Kennedy asked, "Who's Knowles?"

"Care to answer that, Blake?" Caitlin fumed.

"Strat Knowles was a former employee of Outer Limits. He quit to work as a consultant," he returned flatly.

"And?" Caitlin prompted at the silence ensuing when he added nothing further. The group spread out in order to afford each of them a better look at the interior of the cave while Caitlin continued.

"Look, Blake. You've been awfully secretive about Strat, and now here's his bloody suit up here with a pile of gear! What happened to him?"

"I don't know. It's probably just a spare suit."

Kennedy made a spitting noise. "With blood on it? What do you mean you don't know? You said he quit Outer Limits to work as a consultant. What's going on, Blake? If you knew something about what was going on up here that posed a danger to others, you could be held liable for Suzette's death. You know that, right?"

"She wasn't dead yet the last we saw her."

Caitlin made a sound of indignation. "Oh, right, excuse me. How could I forget? You're right, Blake, she's not dead, she's just part of a fucking worm monster being dragged around while her body is being used for...used for oxygen or something..."

At this, Kennedy stepped between the arguing Outer Limits astronauts. "Look, you two. You're talking about a serious situation, and one that, I'm sorry to say, I wouldn't put past Blake. In fact, my spacesuit has the capability to contact our Mission Control in New Mexico directly, but the signal won't penetrate underground. But know this, Blake: if there is some serious wrongdoing on your part, it's up to you how much you want me to use it against you when we get back. You help us out here with this equipment—and so far, at least you've led us to some equipment—but you see this through and get us all back home, and that would go a long, long way to me not using this kind of juicy morsel against you. But right now we don't have the time to get into it, okay? We need to start sorting through that equipment over there and figure out what we can use, what we can take back with us."

Blake stayed silent but the others agreed and Caitlin dropped her line of inquiry, promising Blake she'd revisit the subject later. The double team made their way cautiously to the center of the cave, spreading out around the pile of space gear. They began picking through it to figure out what they had at their disposal, to separate the junk from potentially useful items. After a couple of minutes, Takeo pointed to a metal canister. "Oxygen tank, here. Gauge reads full."

"Another over here," Kennedy called from the other side of the pile, bending down to pick up another cylinder.

"Let's set everything we're going to want right over here, together." Kennedy pointed to a patch of ground a little ways away from the center of the cave and the gear. The astronauts began carrying objects there and depositing them.

"Still looking for that parts box," Blake said, rooting around the stuff. The implication was clear: Black Sky had the most valuable components of what they wanted, in the form of the oxygen cylinders, but what Outer Limits most needed was the electronic part likely to be in that box. Not a minute later, Asami called out. "Got something here, Blake."

She held up a gray metal container.

"Don't open it," Blake cautioned. "We don't want anything to float away." The reminder that there was limited gravity here wasn't likely needed, and yet the image of a critical part floating up and getting caught in some narrow crevice in the cave ceiling or wall was a grim one, indeed.

Kennedy agreed. "Let's just take the whole box back to the lander and open it there. What else can we use?"

The team looked around and scavenged a few more odds and ends, but clearly the big prizes were the full oxygen canisters and the large box of electrical parts. Blake eyeballed his suit's oxygen gauge. "How about we get going, people? I doubt we can carry too much more, anyway."

No objections were voiced. The team rounded up the gear in the center of the cave. They split the burden as equally as possible. Here on the moon, weight was not the issue, simply the bulkiness and unwieldy nature of some of the items. But they managed to grab all of the gear and exit the cave back into the tunnels.

Blake led the way, free of gear so that he could scout ahead to navigate if necessary, with Kennedy behind him, carrying one of the oxygen tanks. Once they got into a hiking rhythm, moving through the trails, things went smoothly. So smoothly, in fact, that Kennedy and Blake got to talking, which was okay for a while, but then, after noticing Blake craning his head around to check the walls and ceilings so frequently, the subject of the creatures came up.

"So, Blake, let me ask you...when exactly did you plan to unveil your discovery of life on the moon? At some opportune moment timed to inflict maximum damage to Black Sky, I suppose, right?"

Blake was indignant. "Believe it or not, Kennedy, but your operation is not the only thing on my mind at all times. I—"

Kennedy whirled around from where he'd been standing to get a closer look at the tunnel wall, concerned that, as he had heard, it wasn't really a wall, to literally point a finger at Blake. As he spun, the valve of the oxygen tank knocked against the wall.

"Blake, the problem with you has always been—" He cut himself off mid-sentence as he felt the tank hit. He stopped to stare at the valve. It was marked with a red line that was visible when in the OFF position, but now the line was green, meaning the valve was open. Behind him, Asami pointed to it.

"Kennedy! Valve's open. Close it!"

The Black Sky CEO reached out and twisted the valve shut, but not before a gush of pure oxygen was released into the airless passage.

33 | THE CONSULTANT

"Asami, did that valve open?" Blake's voice rung with concern.

"It did," Kennedy responded.

"I don't trust you to tell me the truth, Kennedy. Sort of like that time you told me we were getting quality chips from that company in Mongolia. That worked out real well, as I recall—"

"It opened, Blake! I saw it." Asami's shrill words cut Blake off.

"We need to get out of here very fast then, people," Blake said. "Our lab scientist says the creatures are attracted to pure oxygen."

"How does he know that?" Kennedy asked.

"We need to move *now!*" was Blake's only response. The group took off down the tunnel at a loping, bouncing moonwalk, the top of their helmets occasionally scraping against the ceiling.

"Blake, how does your scientist know that the creatures are attracted to oxygen? It's dangerous for us to move this fast through here," Kennedy said, panting, "so I think we have a right to know your reasoning."

But Blake hurried on in silence, pausing at a Y-fork to look left, then spot their footprints and move right. They heard Caitlin's voice next over the comm link.

"He knows because he and Martin Hughes captured a small, live specimen earlier and brought it back to our lander's lab."

At this, Kennedy actually stopped in his tracks despite the well-known urgency for haste. "*What?*"

Takeo bumped into him with his sudden halt.

"Yes, we brought back a specimen to the lab, that's how we know. Can we get going now, please?" Blake came back.

"Sure we can," Kennedy said, putting one foot in front of the other again, "but tell me this, Blake. How many more secrets are you hiding from us? I mean c'mon, it's been one thing after another. Reminds me of the time when you misled our investors into thinking our home security software would be first to market even though you knew a Chinese competitor would beat us. Remember that, Blake? Remember Tsing Mao?"

"I remember it all too well, Kennedy. I also recall that—"

Suddenly, the tunnel wall opened up on their right side. A cavernous, dark space appeared there for a moment but was then filled in as an enormous one of the creatures filed its body past the opening.

"That one is huge!" Takeo said. He sounded genuinely scared.

"What do we do?" Kennedy looked over at Caitlin and Blake.

"Stay calm," Blake told him. "It's very large, it won't be able to enter the tunnel just anywhere. Hopefully it keeps going."

But no sooner had he finished his sentence that the great beast halted its forward movement, sliding to a stop next to the group. Its gray, scaly body quivered in unpredictable spasms.

"It stopped," Caitlin said.

"Maybe we should go," Kennedy suggested.

"Wait, what's that?" Asami pointed to a section of the worm's body, near the underbelly. "There's some kind of discoloration."

Blake stared at it, too. "Does everyone have everything they're supposed to be carrying? Because it looks like this thing may be sitting on something manmade."

Everyone accounted for what they were carrying; nothing was missing. Then the worm moved, rotated inside the rock wall, so that what they had been thinking of as its "belly" now rode up higher within the rock opening.

"Is that—" someone started.

"It's a helmet," Asami said. "Wait..."

"It's a face!" Kennedy suddenly screamed. "Oh my God, it's a face? What is going on here? Blake! Let's go!"

But no one moved. They were too entranced by the horror of what they were witnessing, like a group of motorists rubbernecking at a bad car accident, they couldn't look away.

"It's—is...it?— a helmet with a face in it!" Takeo stammered.

Caitlin dared take a step toward the monstrosity for a better look. She leaned in closer. "It's just a helmet...Wait...*Strat*? Oh my

God, I see his face!" They heard her retching over the comm channel. Blake reached out and thumped her on the back. "Get a grip on yourself, don't throw up. Come on."

Instead, she broke down crying. "What the fuck am I seeing, Blake? Is that... is that Strat?"

Kennedy spoke for Black Sky. "We don't know what he looks like, not that whoever that is, or was, still looks like they used to."

Blake stared into the helmeted face that was sewn into the side of the creature. Through the scratched faceplate, he recognized those green eyes, the shape of the mouth...and...*there*: the scar on the right cheek, fish hook shaped. In New Mexico, Strat had told him the story of how he had gotten it once, as a boy, playing with fireworks one New Year's Eve. *Jesus...*

"Strat!" Caitlin wailed.

They all saw it: the eyes widened in recognition.

"Good lord!" Kennedy gasped. "Where...what happened to his body?"

It was a good question. All they could see was his face.

"It's...it's in there somewhere!" Takeo couldn't hide the incredulity in his voice. "It must be, he's alive! His eyes are open, blinking!"

"But his spacesuit was bloody and shredded back there." Kennedy looked behind them back toward the cave, as if he would see the discarded space garment walking on its own toward them on bloody legs.

"This is like what happened to Suzette," Asami said. A flash of regret coursed through her in an instant as she recalled the uncomfortable incident with the camera. *I'm sorry, Suzette.*

No one replied, and then the worm moved. The face of Strat Knowles was ground into the tunnel floor, the faceplate of his helmet recessed just enough into the creature's flesh to keep it from breaking. A tear ran down Caitlin's face inside her helmet, before the worm righted itself and again Stat's imprisoned head came into view.

This time they saw his lips move. Saw them move and then heard his voice, as if in a nightmare, over the comm channel. Like Suzette's had been, it was bubbly, the words nearly indistinguishable from each other, but barely recognizable.

"Blake...I'm a consultant now..."

Then the worm moved off down the rock fissure it inhabited, carrying Strat with it. They could no longer see him but still they heard his mangled voice. "...moon...I know more about the moon than anyone...moon..."

"Switch channels!" Kennedy demanded. They did, and then they started walking. But soon Strat found them on this new frequency. "...consultant. Need my help. It hurts...pain. I know everything now though."

"He's not making any sense!" Blake yelled. "Let's go!" He and Kennedy led the way through the tunnel, with Caitlin bringing up the rear, constantly looking back to watch for the massive worm— Strat's worm.

Then Asami's shriek pierced their earpieces.

34 | THEY'RE BAAAAACK

Asami was second to last in line in the procession of moonwalkers. Takeo was behind her and Caitlin immediately in front of her. A yawning gulf appeared to their right and a massive worm-like animal jutted into the passage. At first, it slammed its humongous proboscis, if those earthly zoological terms had any meaning here, to and fro, whipping up a highly localized maelstrom of lunar dust and knocking Takeo backwards to land on his side.

Then the worm reared its head up again and an aperture at the end of it dilated, the "mouth" not so much as unhinging on a set of jaws as it was unfolding like an old camera lens. The body of the animal tracked across the tunnel floor while the head bent at an ungodly angle, bringing the aperture down on Asami's helmeted head. It seemed to inhale the spacewoman into its gullet, her feet leaving the ground, flailing ineffectively in the airless void.

"Get me out, get me...Caitlin! Blake...anybody!"

The only part of Asami not yet ingested was from the knees down. Caitlin was closest to her and the first to grab hold of her feet. She crossed Asami's ankles and clutched them together so as to get a better grip, but the sheer force of the monster was overwhelming, and Caitlin was shipped into the tunnel ceiling as the worm-creature twisted spasmodically about. From her awkward position lying pressed up against the tunnel roof, Caitlin lashed out with a booted foot and kicked the creature in its...underside, she guessed it was. The flesh was soft and spongy, though, absorbing most of her impact as if she had booted a half-deflated rubber ball. Even so, the animal gyrated even more with her efforts, twisting and cavorting recklessly as the comm channel filled with panicky shouts.

By the time Caitlin hit the ground in that slow motion moon gravity and looked up again, the other astronauts were doing battle with the thing, lashing out at it with small hand tools, coordinating their efforts to attack different parts of the beast. But what captured her attention was Asami. Somehow she had inverted herself within the beasts' mouth so that her head was now visible. Caitlin made eye contact with her through their faceplates, and in that ephemeral burst of wordless human communication, she stared into depths of terror that had been unknown to her only moments before, for the alien being's jaws or mouth or whatever the hell it had began to close around Asami's head.

"Need help, people!" Caitlin pleaded. The group was already circled tightly around the worm-thing, poking and prodding at it to little effect. And then the animal's fleshy outer lip-like appendages sloshed over Asami's helmet, the astronaut looking out as they swiped back and forth over the glass, like a scared kid in a carwash. Then the sea of swampy flesh inside the animal's mouth circulated, moved, parted, revealing a set of teeth in multiple rows. Not sharp teeth like fangs or even incisors, but more like big molars with flat, grinding surfaces.

Those teeth closed around Asami's helmet with ferocious speed and force, cutting off the astronaut's scream as the helmet shattered, instantly exposing her head to the zero-pressure environment. Her head imploded, caving in on itself in a microsecond. The creature reared back and gyrated with the influx of bio-fluids down its open maw while the faceplates of Kennedy and Blake were splattered with gore to the point it obscured their vision.

"Go, c'mon!" somebody said. The point was clear. Asami was dead for sure now, there was nothing they could do for her, and so unless they wanted to be next, it was time to get out of here. Caitlin fell into line behind Takeo, who scrambled to wriggle his way around the creature into the open tunnel, down which Blake and Kennedy were already tripping and loping and tumbling. They moved any way they could to put distance between themselves and the specter of death that had claimed Asami.

In his struggle to keep up, Takeo tripped and let go of the other oxygen canister, sending it tumbling over Caitlin's head and back toward the creature which now sat in a loose pile blocking the tunnel, quivering with digestive effort.

The canister sailed over Caitlin's outstretched arm and she had to watch it tumble onto the tunnel floor on the other side of the mammoth, amorphous beast. She looked on as a river of Asami's blood sluiced down the alien hide before turning back toward the group. Takeo met her gaze, as if to acknowledge the severity of his mistake. They had lost fifty percent of their precious new oxygen supply. More than that including the leak from Kennedy's tank. But it was a matter of live as best you could with half of the supply or die trying to get the other half. Caitlin wasn't ready to die, and so she moved away from the creature down the tunnel.

But Takeo stood his ground staring at the engorged animal.

"What are you doing? C'mon!" Caitlin called.

"I can get it. I—" He broke off as the worm-beast rolled on the ground, a ripple of weird flesh trembling in waves up and down its body.

"No, Takeo! Don't—look, they're coming!" Caitlin pointed past him, where the big worm had curled itself into a tight ball, leaving a narrow gap between itself and the tunnel wall. Past it they could see a river of the smaller creatures—most the size of rats but a few more like footballs, undulating through the regolith, heading their way en masse.

The astronaut saw that Caitlin was right and he gave up on saving his pride, not to mention his oxygen. He turned and loped off down the tunnel, where the others were now out of sight around a bend. Caitlin followed after him, finding it difficult to keep from bouncing into the walls and ceiling when taking the longer strides used in running. She had experience moon walking, not moon running, as did they all.

She caught up to the rest of the group as they emerged from the tunnel system into the interior of the crater. They were farther down toward the crater floor than the tunnel they entered earlier with Suzette, though, and so had a longer hike to the rim. Caitlin tried not to look down, tried to simply put one foot in front of the other until she was far up the crater, but she hadn't even reached the next tunnel entrance when she looked behind her and below.

And there they were: a veritable horde of the creatures, burrowing their way up the crater along with them. Moving *fast*, too, Caitlin noticed. "Step on it, guys, these things are coming after us and they're making good time!"

The comm loop was punctuated with heavy grunting and pants as the team loped and clawed their way up the inside of the crater. A couple of times someone tripped and fell, bouncing at an awkward angle until someone else pulled them back up. Progress was made but it became clear that the creatures were even faster. At the current rate, they would be overrun by the space animals before they reached the lip of the crater.

Caitlin couldn't imagine what the thousands of small creatures would do to them, but she didn't want to imagine that, especially after not having to imagine the fates of Asami and Suzette. Of the two, she supposed Asami had the more enviable fate, being killed quickly. She found herself wondering why Suzette still lived and then forced herself not to think about it. There was no time. Not if she wanted to live herself.

She yelled into her comm unit. "Need to do something, guys. Those things are gaining on us."

"We could split up," Kennedy suggested. "Take different routes to the lander."

No one disagreed, and with the shuffling of the lunar dirt growing closer to them, Blake said he and Kennedy would head off to the left and up, while Caitlin and Takeo would go right and up.

"At the very least," Blake said, "even if these things follow both of our new groups, they'll have to split their numbers in order to do it."

Just as Caitlin uttered her agreement with the new direction, she caught a boot on a rock and went floating horizontally until she impacted with a boulder. Takeo helped to right her and urged her to get going. "They're almost to us," he said, voice unemotional.

"Damn these things are quick," they heard Kennedy say, from his part of the slope. They all continued their hard-scrabble ascent, zigzagging at times in an attempt to throw the creatures off. It didn't seem to, since the pack of dirt dwellers continued in a straight line for as long as they had to and then adjusted accordingly once they picked up a scent or a signal or whatever it was that enabled them to hone in on the humans.

Caitlin and Takeo were about twenty feet from the rim of the crater when they heard Blake's voice issuing an expletive, followed by Kennedy telling him to calm down.

"What is it?" Caitlin demanded while bunny-hopping over a large depression in the ground.

"The parade of these animals is still making its way from the crater to the LEM," said Blake.

"Is that where the ones that have been chasing us are going?" Caitlin reached the lip of the crater at the same time as her new colleague. She looked out over the lunar plain and instantly saw what Blake was talking about. Yes, there was a flood of creatures as there had been before when they left the LEM, but now there were very large individuals—perhaps even as big as the ones that had consumed Asami and Suzette in the caves—interspersed with the junior variety. When these behemoths moved, clouds of dust eased away from the ground ahead of their passage.

"At least they're still pretty much in a straight line," Caitlin said. She glanced back down into the crater, where the avalanche of smallish worms tunneled through the soil, perhaps a minute away from reaching her.

"Down we go, c'mon." Takeo jumped off the crater lip, bounding down the crater's outer slope in high leaps with long, arcing trajectories. After a quick look back at the deluge of rampaging alien mass, Caitlin also leapt down the crater, eyeing the Black Sky lunar lander on the flat plain in the distance and the moon buggy at the foot of the hill.

They heard occasional shouts from Blake and Kennedy as they made their way down, fighting their own mini-battles as they navigated their part of the slope. "Watch it! Look out for that—no...there! Go..."

Near the bottom of the crater, Caitlin was enveloped in a cloud of moon dust. At first she thought her companion was behind her, kicking it down on her after one of the many rough tumbles they took during their descent, but when it cleared a little she saw him ten feet in front of her, angling towards the rover. So what had caused it? She craned her neck around for a look.

A massive worm reared up above her, a ring of tendrils each several feet long, surrounding its mouth opening. "Move, Takeo!"

she cried out, attempting to motivate herself more than anything. With a great sense of relief, she saw Blake hop into the rover's driver seat and power it up.

Kennedy was tossing a large boulder in slow motion at a squat worm the size of a compact car. As soon as he lobbed it, he wheeled and ran for the rover without waiting to see if he had hit his target. As Caitlin ran for the rover, she saw the big rock land squarely atop the creature's tubular upper body, where it disappeared into its copious folds without dropping back to the ground, as if the being had simply absorbed the heavy projectile.

A cascade of smaller animals continued to slide down the crater toward them. All of the team reached the rover and climbed in. Blake put the vehicle into gear and accelerated out onto the flat lunar plain. At first, the momentum of the oncoming horde was such that the animals kept pace with the car, only a few feet back. But as the seconds ticked on, it became clear that the beasts were not able to close the gap. Surprisingly fast as they were, they could not travel through and over the ground faster than the rover at its top speed.

Suddenly, an alarm brayed from the cockpit of the vehicle. Blake narrowed his eyes at a blinking red LED.

"What is that?" Kennedy asked what they all wanted to know.

"Battery overheat alarm," Blake reported. "Never had it come on before."

"Probably due to the sustained top speed," Caitlin said, craning her neck around to monitor the creatures' progress. "You could ease back a hair, but not much more than that the way these things are coming at us. They are *fast*."

Blake did that to take the strain off the batteries and Caitlin watched as the worm tribe narrowed the rover's lead by ever so much. By the time they were half way across the plain to Kennedy's lander, though, the creatures had fallen back some, unable to maintain the shocking speed over long distances. All four riders bounced around crazily in the rig as Blake propelled them across the plain, the wheels dipping into small depressions occasionally, sending Takeo flying up into space at one point, holding onto a tubular frame rail by one hand before being pulled back in by Caitlin.

As they neared the lander, a new danger appeared. The rover crossed over the line of animals that had already been making its way to the LEM, scattering them momentarily. But as Caitlin looked back in the wake of the crossing, she saw them reorganize and join the newer path of following creatures, and together the two streams of animals plowed after the rover as it drove up to the lunar lander.

"Out, out, out, everybody out!" Blake yelled as he applied the buggy's brakes. Kennedy transmitted on the frequency to his crew in the LEM.

"Incoming, open the airlock, we're at the front door, over!"

They heard an acknowledgement as they fell out of the vehicle and made giant steps over to the LEM's airlock. Caitlin could see from the way the creatures piled up on the side of the craft that the oxygen leak had still not been fixed. The team, slowed somewhat by the equipment they had salvaged, ran up to the outer airlock door just as it slid open.

"In! They're almost here..." Caitlin pointed to the oncoming rush of turbulent moon flesh. A large animal pushed a compliment of smaller ones ahead of it like a bow wave in front of a seagoing vessel. The moonwalkers piled inside the airlock and the outer door slid closed just as the creatures reached the LEM.

From inside, they watched the door bulge slightly with the onslaught of the rushing life forms.

35 | DILEMMA

Outer Limits Lunar Lander

"I'm not sure that 'body disposal' is among those things in my list of duties for this flight." James Burton narrowed his eyes at Dallas from behind the plastic safety glasses he wore as they stood over Martin's dead body. Dallas gave him a pleading look. A look that said, 'I'm trying to work with you, here, rather than one of dissatisfaction or intimidation."

"Look, Mr. Burton, I know that. Believe me, this is the last thing I was hoping to have you get involved with, but it's much safer to have two people carry his body outside than one. Can you please just help me out so we can get his corpse out of here and not wait to see what happens once he starts to decompose?"

That had an effect. Burton said nothing but averted his gaze from Dallas' to that of the semi-translucent corpse on the lab table. Checking that his spacesuit was secure one last time, James snapped his helmet into place, to avoid having to do it later once they were carrying the body, and because it would keep him from breathing in any contaminants or fatal fluids on Martin's body. He bent to the task of lifting the dead exobiologist. Dallas did the same and they hefted the body.

"Try to avoid it coming into contact with any surfaces," Dallas cautioned. "We don't want to contaminate anything."

"I got him, let's go." Burton had the corpse by the legs while Dallas hefted him from the chest. They shuffled out of the lab and into the main working area of the spaceship. They were making their way across when Blake's voice erupted from the radio, tinged with urgency. Dallas threw his head back in frustration; they had just gotten into a workable rhythm carrying the dead body, and now they would have to set it down. Dallas listened for a few seconds while he and James still held Martin's corpse above the floor, but Blake's message required attention.

"Set him down." Dallas ran to the radio after they dropped Martin unceremoniously to the floor.

"...I said, DO YOU READ ME?"

Dallas scooped up the transmitter. "Dallas here, Blake. I read you loud and clear, over."

"Good. Listen carefully, please. Caitlin and I are transmitting from Black Sky's lander."

"Excellent! So you got there and they let you in. I assume they let you in, right? You're not still standing outside knocking on the door, are you?" Dallas turned around to smile at James, who had backed away from Martin's corpse. He was paying close attention to the radio call but did not return Dallas' grin.

"Caitlin and I are inside the lander, Dallas."

"What about Asami—where's she?"

The frequency seemed to go dead. Dallas furrowed his brow. "Blake?"

"Asami didn't make it out of the tunnels." He proceeded to recount the events of their moonwalk, while James listened with his face gradually transforming into increasingly horrified expressions. James was stricken with as much grief as one could have for knowing someone so short a time, flashing on her gloved hand holding his as they stood outside the lander.

When Blake had finished relaying what had happened, he asked Dallas how the repairs to the ship were going. Dallas shook his head even though he knew Blake couldn't see him. "I can't make further headway without that part, the actuator—did you find one?"

"That's a negative, Dallas. We did recover the box of parts that was left behind in the tunnels, but Caitlin combed through it already and there's no actuator in there, repeat no actuator found, over."

"Are any of the parts you found helpful?"

"We did find a part to fix Black Sky's ship."

"So what about them—do they have the part we need? Can you make a trade?"

"They don't have it. Well, that's not entirely true. They do have one actuator—the one that's working and in use now. But without it, their ship would be unable to function, too."

"So...let me make sure I'm hearing this right... To save one ship is to sacrifice the other, is that what I'm hearing?"

"Unfortunately, that is the situation as it now stands, Dallas. Unless something develops to change that, but..."

"But our oxygen and battery power will only last so long."

Blake did not respond to this. He didn't need to. It was the truth, their reality. Dallas continued. "Okay...it sounds like Black Sky's lander is closer to being operational than ours is, since they have the parts they need."

"And they have one additional oh-two canister, yes."

"All right, so because we've..." Dallas shook his head and seemed to choke back his words a little as he turned to face away from James, whose stare was unwavering as he watched the conversation unfold. "As tragic as it is, because we've lost three people—Martin's dead, too— I think we might be able to fit all of us in Black Sky's craft for the return trip to one of the command modules. What do you think?"

Sounds of commotion issued over the communication channel. Blake's voice came back sounding harried and stressed. "Probably. Listen, they're close to fixing the oxygen leak here with that new part, but because it leaked for so long, there's a large horde of the creatures around the ship. Something's banging out there now and I've got to go help if I can."

The first hint of worry crept into Dallas' voice as it dawned on him that he and James were a long way from the others in the craft that was most likely to be working soon. He avoided eye contact with the FAA monitor as he transmitted to Blake before he could sign off. "It's too far for us to walk over there, Blake. If we combine crews into Black Sky's LEM, how do we get over there, over?"

There was a disconcerting moment where a series of clicks were broadcast, leading Dallas to believe Blake had signed off or simply left the transmitter hanging, but then the CEO's voice came back through the speaker. "I'll send Caitlin in the rover to pick you up. By doing that, she might be able to draw the creatures away from the ship long enough for us to make the serious repairs. The rovers are faster than the creatures, fortunately, although I wish I didn't know that firsthand."

"Sounds like a working plan." Dallas was relieved. He didn't really know Blake all that well, as a person, and he wasn't sure what kind of moral compass the man possessed. His business instincts were known for being positively ruthless, of course, but that was just business. *Wasn't it?*

"It is, but we'll need a much larger distraction than that if we are to get the craft off the ground without interference from the worms. I've really got to go, but let me outline the plan for that so you can bring the items we'll need from our ship on the rover." He didn't want to mention it, but Dallas was relieved to hear that he had things Blake wanted, which would make it that much more likely he sends Caitlin back in the rover.

Blake proceeded to describe the plan, at the end of which Dallas sighed heavily. It was very dicey, full of what-ifs and multiple variables like landmines in a field of uncertainty. But if everything went just so, it might possibly work.

Then a reverberant clanging noise emanated from the speaker and Blake shouted, "Over and out, Dallas!"

36 | BAIT...

Black Sky Lunar Lander

Caitlin snapped her helmet on with a finality that both unnerved and energized her. This was it. They had a plan, they were executing it, and she was a key element of that execution. If she couldn't drive that rover to the Outer Limits LEM, then Dallas and James would likely perish, left behind on the barren moon.

Takeo escorted her to the airlock. He said he felt like they'd been through a lot together already and that making sure she would be able to drive off in the rover would be easy by comparison. Everyone else was in the middle of repairing the ship. Even with Black Sky's needed part and the new oxygen cylinder, the work itself was painstakingly slow going, and there was no room for error. Time had also been lost to an EVA in order to fend a few of the worms off of critical parts of the ship. They had stayed away for a while, but now seemed to be returning in most aggressive fashion.

Takeo donned his helmet. "I'll go with you to help you get to the rover. After that, you're on your own until you get back here. Good luck." He smiled at her and she wondered if he had some kind of attraction to her as a result of their bonding on the trip back from the tunnels.

"Thanks. I'll take all the help I can get." With that, the outer airlock door slid open and they stepped out onto the moon together.

Immediately, Caitlin registered a blur of movement out of her peripheral vision and then felt a thud on her facemask. A smear of blue liquid marred the glass surface after a small worm bounced off. The suit helmets were not equipped with "windshield wipers," a feature that had been discussed but dismissed as being unnecessary.

"They're falling from the roof." Takeo pointed to the top of his LEM. A horde of animals toppled off the side of the spacecraft like lemmings from a cliff, splashing onto the ground and kicking up dust-devils wherever they happened to land. Caitlin made a giant stride toward the rover, parked perhaps twenty-five feet away. She wished now that they'd driven all the way to the airlock, though, because between her and the rover was a river of worms still leading from the crater to the ship.

They walked up to it and she judged whether she'd be able to jump over the fast-flowing stream of life. It would be close. Small creatures were ejected from the main plume with regularity, spouting up into the airless atmosphere. Still, there was no other way around. But her companion had an idea.

"Here," he said getting down on one knee as he bashed a creature away from his helmet. "You step on my gloves and I'll give you a boost. Get you up higher before you jump."

Caitlin thought it could work. With a little extra height and springboard power, she might just be able to launch herself over the river of creatures. Takeo wasn't going with her, so he wouldn't have to worry about how to cross over himself.

She placed her right foot in the crux of his interlaced fingers and pressed down, prepping him for the force of her coming jump. Off to their left, one of the football-sized animals broke from the river of life and wobbled toward them, only a few feet away.

"I'm ready, do it!" Takeo said, one eye on the advancing threat.

Caitlin eyeballed the ground on the other side of the oxygen-seeking worms and then launched herself. In midair over the creatures, she felt a pattering sensation on the soles of her boots as the smaller animals pelted her like rain from the ground. Due to the low gravity, she was able to achieve a much higher jump than if she had been earthbound, and she sailed over the moving line of creatures, landing on the other side.

"Go!" her companion encouraged her. The animals were still drawn as if inexorably toward the oxygen leak on the LEM, but there was no point in Caitlin standing around to see if they would take an interest in her before she even got to the rover. She bounded off in the now familiar hopping moon run toward the rover. When she got to it, she jumped in without looking back and hit the power button.

The control panel lit up and Caitlin put the vehicle into drive. She wasn't looking forward to what she was about to do. She'd much rather simply drive over to her LEM and pick up Dallas and James, but if she wanted to make sure they'd have a ship to return to that could get them home again, she had to draw the worms off Black Sky's lander.

She accelerated away from the line of animals, testing the rover, making sure it was working properly; warming it up until the controls were but an extension of her hands as she coaxed the maximum performance out of the machine. When she felt as ready as possible, she put the buggy into a turn until she was pointed back at the LEM—and the stream of moving flesh. She drove toward the animals at full speed, watching the Black Sky man bounce-run back toward the LEM.

She eyed the movement carefully as she was jolted along, looking for a spot to impact where there were none of the larger individuals. She was pretty sure she could run over the smaller ones, but she didn't want to take a chance with the larger ones fouling up the drivetrain. When she saw a suitable target, she hunched lower in the seat and focused on maintaining a stable trajectory.

She had no idea what driving through the animals would do—if it would have no real effect, where they simply reorganized once the interruption was over, or if they would abandon their well-formed line to chase the rover around. But she had to try something to give them a chance to work outside the LEM without the threat of the beasts, if only for a little while.

Caitlin plowed the rover through the line of burrowing aliens at a near perpendicular angle, sloughing them out from under the wire wheels as it cut through. She felt the vehicle bog down for a second and her hands white-knuckled the steering wheel, anticipating getting stuck in the middle of the animal activity and wondering what she would do. She lurched forward again and saw the front wheels kick up a flurry of dust. This was followed by a bump as the rear tires banged over a thick clump of worms and then the moon buggy was rolling over flat ground once more.

She had done it—broken through the flow of creatures without damaging the rover or getting it stuck. She set the moon car into a turn toward the LEM.

"Good work! You broke them up," she heard Takeo say into the comm unit. "The really good news is, they're not heading for the LEM anymore."

"What's the bad news?" Caitlin slowed as she turned the wheel some more.

"They're coming after you."

"Fast?"

"Affirmative."

"Let me see what I can do about the ones on the side of the ship."

"Copy that." He lurked nearby the airlock in case the creatures became too aggressive, while Caitlin turned the corner around the spacecraft. She sucked in her breath as she took in the massive conglomeration of seething, writhing animals that literally wormed their way up the side of the ship, huddling en masse in an oxygen-fueled frenzy. Caitlin considered simply ramming them with the buggy, which had a decent front fender, but decided she couldn't risk any more damage to the spaceship. She would have to be careful and clip the outside of the group and hope that deterred them.

She increased her speed and pulled hard to the right as she passed the huddle of vermiform intruders. She noticed that, unlike those in the line, these animals paid no attention to her or her vehicle at all as they gorged on the chemical rush leaking from the ship. It was like they were drunk on oxygen, or perhaps blood lusting like a shark in a feeding frenzy. Whatever it was, she would have to do more if she was to disturb them.

"Where are the ones from the line—coming this way?" she transmitted to Takeo.

"They're confused. They chase after me, then turn toward the side of the lander, then back toward me again. It's like they don't know what to do. I'll stay on this side of the ship, though, so I don't lead them your way."

"Copy that. I don't need any more than I've already got here. So many of them..."

She trailed off as she banked into a turn in order to come back for another pass at the huge mountain of worms threatening to envelope the ship. This time she approached closer to the pileup, still at a parallel course, driving by them, swiping a few with the side rail as she passed. Looking back as she carved out a turn, she saw some of the creatures tumbling from the pile and then rolling around on the ground. She had disrupted them somewhat.

She came around for another pass, executing on it the same way as the first. More minor success. She repeated it again and again, and with each pass more of the animals ended up wriggling around on the ground in disjointed fashion rather than glomming onto the station where they prevented access to the leaking oxygen port.

The Black Sky astronaut walked around the corner. "It's working! Keep it up!" Takeo radioed the crew inside to get ready to make the repairs. Caitlin continued making rover passes, crunching over the smaller animals while avoiding the larger ones as she side-swiped the wormy dogpile. When it became apparent that there were more animals on the ground than on the lander, she drove the rover in a wide arc away from the LEM.

"Think you can take it from here?" Caitlin asked Takeo.

"Roger that. You thinned 'em out for us, thanks."

"All right. I'm off to pick up our new crew."

"Good luck!" Takeo watched as Caitlin drove off toward the Outer Limits lunar lander.

37 | ... AND SWITCH

Caitlin drove toward the river of creatures she had dislocated earlier by driving through their midst. By now they had come back together, resuming their organizational drive as they plowed toward the LEM.

"Better make that repair work in a hurry," she radioed Takeo. "The ones coming from the crater look like they're about to be on the move again. She slowed the rover to a stop to get a look at them. At least now she was already on the other side—the side closest to the Outer Limits lander, so she didn't have to worry about crossing through them again. But my, oh my, Caitlin thought as she scanned the line of beasts. There were some large individuals here. One she estimated to be the size of a small farm tractor. An animal that size could easily damage the LEM simply by rolling into the side of it as the other, smaller ones had done.

In an attempt to draw it off, she rolled up to it and stopped. The worm, its upper half protruding from the soil, stopped moving and coiled its length so that its head was pointed in Caitlin's direction. She contemplated ramming it, to send it a real message, but decided against it. What if it enveloped her vehicle in its pliable folds? The image of Suzette, hopelessly and permanently intertwined with the creature—embedded into its own physiology—returned to haunt her and she backed off. But she noticed that the giant creature moved in her direction. She waited for it to creep up on her a little closer, then wheeled off a safe distance away. She continued this process until she looked back to the line of worms and saw she had effectively lured the largest among them almost a football field away.

She began driving the rover toward the Outer Limits LEM, not at full speed, for she didn't want to outrun the worm, leaving it to go back to the precious Black Sky craft. Plus, she'd conserve battery power by not running at top speed. So she drove on at a middling pace, the worm shuffling after her out of curiosity, she supposed. She wasn't sure if it just wasn't moving as fast as it could, or if the large ones couldn't propel themselves as quickly as their diminutive brethren. But regardless, she kept a close watch on the animal in her rear view mirror as she motored on toward her LEM.

She also kept an eye out for new creatures as she went, but didn't see any. At about the midpoint between the two LEMs, the large worm dropped back and when she could no longer see it, she increased her speed. She didn't know if the worm would bury itself where it ended up, or try to make its way back to the rich oxygen source of the Black Sky lander, but she had done her job of drawing it off the site so they could work.

Now she had to complete the other half of her job: pick up Dallas and James and bring them back over to Black Sky. She navigated a rough section of uneven terrain, forcing her to reduce speed, but when she emerged from it onto a flat plain, she should see the Outer Limits LEM in the distance. She checked the mirror to see if the massive worm had used the rough terrain as an opportunity to gain on her, but she saw only a static, gray landscape.

She put the rover to high speed and gripped the steering wheel as she jostled along over the lunar surface. Before long, the boxy form of the LEM took shape. She slowed as she approached, scoping it out visually. The lights were on, indicating they still had power. That was good. Other than that, she didn't see much, no one on an EVA...and then she noticed something on the ground a short distance from the spacecraft. A worm? That was her first thought. But as she rolled nearer in the rover, it soon became apparent that it was not one of the creatures. Not one of the lunar creatures, anyway. It was a creature all right—but a human one. Naked, without a spacesuit, so obviously dead. She rolled closer to the inert form until she could get a detailed look.

The corpse of Martin Hughes lay on the moon. His skin appeared to be a strange color to her, but she couldn't be sure that wasn't due to the unusual ambient lunar light, so bright with no atmosphere to filter the sun this time of day. She guessed that he must have been removed by Dallas in order to reduce risk of biocontamination, since he had been killed by somehow coming into contact with the bio-specimen. Still, she found it unnerving to stare at the dead man on the moon, so much so that she avoided looking at him while she brought the rover to a stop and walked to the airlock.

Inside the lander, she found Dallas and James at the radio console, attempting without success to establish contact with Mission Control. "...dust storm status. Do you read, over?"

Dallas looked up at Caitlin as she approached, her suit helmet now off.

"How was the drive?"

At this, she couldn't help but laugh. "You make it sound as though I was coming up I-95 to stay for the weekend. *Oh, it wasn't too bad, the usual traffic...*"

"The perks of having the only vehicle on the planet, I guess. Plenty of places to park."

"Yeah, except for where the corpses are. And the killer worms. They're having a bitch of a time over at the other LEM, Dallas. I—"

Suddenly Blake's' voice burst through the radio speaker. "Dallas, you copy?"

Dallas turned away from Caitlin to concentrate on the radio. "We read you loud and clear, Blake. Caitlin just got here, over."

"Tell her she did a good job—at first we were able to work outside the LEM on repairing the oxygen leak and damage to the ship's exterior, but those things are back now and we haven't fully made the repairs yet."

Dallas looked back at Caitlin before replying over the radio to Blake. "Maybe when James and I get over there with Caitlin, the extra manpower will make a difference." *We can hope, right?*

"Plus, I'll be able to use the rover again to draw them off once more if necessary," Caitlin added. Dallas relayed this to Blake, who agreed. Then they heard shouting coming from the Black Sky end of the transmission before Blake's voice came gain.

"I better let you get to work. Don't forget to charge the rover fully and bring anything we can use over here that you can fit in the rover. See you soon, over and out."

Dallas signed off and addressed Caitlin and James, who had started to grill the female astronaut on what the situation was like over at Black Sky's ship. "How much strife is there between Blake and Kennedy?"

"You can tell they're uncomfortable around one another but at this point they seem to be working together well enough. They got through the EVA together to get the supplies, so they should be okay."

"What about my counterpart over there, the illustrious Mr. Stenson—how's he doing?"

"Do I detect a hint of sarcasm there, James?"

Burton nodded. "Let's just say I would have been promoted a lot earlier without him around for so long. But I have to admit, all that seems like a minor annoyance compared to what's going on up here."

"Will you be able to work with him if you have to?"

"From what I hear, Blake and Kennedy make Stenson and I look like best friends. We'll be fine."

Caitlin told him about Stenson's openly critical attack on Kennedy's methods, which elicited a knowing smirk from James, although he remained silent.

Dallas jumped down from his control panel seat and moved to put on his spacesuit. "We should get a move on. Caitlin, is the rover charging?"

"First thing I did when I got here was to plug it in."

"Good. How about oxygen? We should have one canister left. Go ahead and grab it while James and I get our suits on, please. Then I've got a little plan to tell you about."

Caitlin found the full oxygen cylinder—now free to use since they would be leaving their ship behind—and loaded it into the rover. Again, she avoided making eye contact with the nude corpse of Martin Hughes. She wondered if he had found some kind of peace, God or no God. When she got back into the LEM, she found Dallas and James fully suited up, but still in the main cabin of the ship. She addressed them through the comm loop.

"I put the oh-two cylinder and a few tools in the rover. Nothing else I can think of. You ready?"

Dallas looked up at her, his fingers poised over a switch. "Just about. Rover's charged and ready to roll?"

"All set."

"Good. Because once we vent the air from this puppy, there's no turning back. And we're likely to have company if we stick around too long."

"Vent the air? Why do that? I know we don't intend to use this ship, but still..."

"That's the plan I was telling you about. To see if we can attract the creatures over in this direction, take some of the pressure off of the Black Sky lander."

"That will probably add pressure to our drive over there, though." Caitlin flashed on driving over the squishy worms.

"You got here, though. So it's doable." This from James, who usually remained silent to observe the interplay among the astronauts, but now deciding that his own future was less than certain, asserting his opinion.

Both astronauts stared at him as though they had witnessed a dog speak English. Dallas recovered first. "Mr. Burton has a point."

Caitlin pointed through the ship walls to the Black Sky LEM. "They have a relatively small leak, though—one that over days leaked a substantial amount of oxygen, but you're talking about suddenly releasing the entire volume of air in the ship? That'll be like ringing a dinner bell. I can't say for sure how many of these things will be attracted to that and how aggressive they're likely to be."

Dallas withdrew his hand from the first of the switches necessary to begin the venting process. "I'll leave it up to you, Caitlin."

James' eyes widened as he looked from Dallas to Caitlin, who walked up to the switch. "I suppose once we get over there, we're going to need every edge we can get. Give me a three minute head start to get out to the rover and get it started up."

Dallas consulted his wristwatch while she made her way to the airlock. After an uncomfortable three minutes during which James Burton made frequent eye contact with him through their faceplates but said nothing, Dallas' hands got busy on the control console. He executed the series of actions required to open the valve that vented the LEM's cabin air supply to space, flooding the moon with gasses the barren world would ordinarily never be exposed to.

A red flashing light went off and Dallas stood. "Party's over here. Let's get over to our new home on the moon, shall we?" With that, he and James exited the craft. With a last look at Martin's lifeless body—soon to be worm food, Dallas reflected—they moved quickly to the rover, where Caitlin waited at the controls as promised. Dallas took the front passenger seat while James climbed in back.

Caitlin put the buggy into gear. "Fasten your seatbelts, boys. I have a feeling this is gonna be one helluva ride."

38 | FIGHT

They didn't speak much in the rover. Caitlin was focused on driving and following her own rover tracks back to Black Sky's LEM while Dallas and James obsessively monitored the landscape for signs of the creatures, knowing they had baited them with oxygen. They had gone almost halfway and still seen nothing out of the ordinary. But Just as Dallas was about to question the effectiveness of the deliberate air-leak, Caitlin slowed the rover gradually until she came to a complete stop.

"What's up?" James said from the back seat, looking all about. Caitlin pointed straight ahead. "Ground's moving up ahead. See that?"

Ripples of motion stirred the lunar floor in the distance.

"Still pretty far away," Dallas commented.

Caitlin nodded. "Could mean they're big ones. Really big."

"Can we go around them?" James asked, a quiver of fear in his voice.

"I can try. No point just sitting around waiting for them to get to us." Caitlin put the rover back into gear and angled left, taking them off the path they had been on. She drove without mishap until reaching the area where they'd sighted the disturbance. Although they were off to the left of it, immediately they could see that the upheaval was occurring over a very large area, and not simply in "the road" they had chosen based on the rover's previous tracks.

"They're here, too," she said, slowing the rover.

James' voice made her jump. "There's one behind us! Go!"

Caitlin glanced into the rear view mirror and saw one of the gargantuan slug-like beasts burrowing into the ground, then rising out of it again, porpoising through the soil like a dolphin in slow motion. She set the vehicle into forward motion again, knowing that not far in front of them was an entire underground wall of the frenzied alien animals.

And then James yelled again, something unintelligible this time, but it mattered little what he actually said. She looked back through the mirror and saw the massive worm animal jump through the airless void as if attempting to land on the moon buggy. She made a sharp right and the creature landed where the rover had been mere seconds earlier, thudding into the ground with a spray of gray dust.

"Watch it: one o'clock." Dallas' voice was calm and low. Caitlin eyeballed the direction he indicated and there—perhaps forty feet away—another humongous worm-thing reared up out of the soil. Dozens of little ones wriggled around its fleshy, waddling base, like drops of water into a lake. Caitlin veered left, wishing to steer well-clear of that one. But as soon as she did, a barrier of medium-sized animals cropped up, perhaps the size of bean bags. They rolled along, easily as high as the rover and in some cases piled two or three individuals high.

She veered back to the right, but the sudden maneuvering caused the rover to fishtail, and when she hit the hippo-sized worm that suddenly breached out of the soil, the vehicle was already unstable. The beast pushed up and out of the ground beneath the left front wheel, flipping the moon buggy onto its side.

The web harnesses kept the vehicle's occupants inside the rover, which was good since the moon buggy was ringed with snuffling worms of various sizes. Dallas was first to unhook his harness and scramble out of the car. James managed to crawl out on his own, but Caitlin was suspended in the driver seat, which was on the side not in contact with the ground.

She got her harness unclipped and Dallas began pulling her out through the upended side of the vehicle, rather than let her fall to the ground and risk damaging her suit.

"Hurry!" James sounded panicked. "They're all around us!"

Caitlin lifted one leg out through the doorless vehicle, then the other, and Dallas set her onto the moon feet first. Then both of them turned around to see what they were facing.

It wasn't good.

A thick ring of animals surrounded the upturned rover, with a few creatures already inside the ring.

"Look for gaps!" Dallas commanded, head on a swivel as he scanned the perimeter of animals for a weak point. He'd looked almost all the way around when he spotted small one. Maybe a two-foot gap, but it was the weakest point. "Let's go. There!"

He led the three of them toward the opening but the animals closed it off before they had even gone four steps. He looked around the circle again for another opening. Found one, even smaller than the last time, in the opposite direction on the other side of the rover.

"We could tip the rover back and try to drive out!" Caitlin suggested.

James was all for that suggestion, already putting his hands on the vehicle while bracing his feet against the moon.

"I'm afraid to turn my back to these things!" Dallas uttered. "See if you two can right it while I keep an eye on them."

Caitlin got into position alongside James on the other end of the rover. Together, they started to push. Even in the weak gravity of the moon, the rover was still a small car and not all that light for two people to lift. While they pushed it, a worm the same height as a medium sized dog, but much longer, rolled sideways toward Dallas, its gristly proboscis opening and closing as it went.

Dallas was caught by surprise at how fast it moved. He attempted a high jump as it rolled up to him, and while his right foot cleared the worm, his left tripped up on its upper surface, knocking him onto the creature's fleshy topside.

"Need help!" Dallas managed as he fell off the worm while it rolled on without him. Caitlin turned to look back at Dallas and she lost her grip on the rover, causing it to knock into her and James.

"Watch it!" the FAA man shouted. "Push up!" But the momentum was too much and the car fell back on them, upside down. Meanwhile, Dallas rolled off the worm he landed on, sprawling onto the moon's flat surface. He moved to right himself but the creatures converged on him, smothering him while he was still on his hands and knees.

"Caitlin!"

But it was James Burton who reached him first. He lashed out with a foot, delivering a vicious kick to a large animal slithering over Dallas' neck. The creature recoiled, its reactive wriggling atop Dallas' back flattening the astronaut to the ground. Then Caitlin arrived and delivered another kick to the same worm, this time causing it to slither away from Dallas.

Burton whirled back around and ran to the rover, trying to right it himself. "They're closing in! C'mon, let's get this thing going!"

Caitlin was about to help him when the ground opened up right in front of her. Dallas was in the process of pushing up with his arms to get his feet, when suddenly he fell into the open, gooey maw of a strange worm. While substantial, it was not nearly as big as the one that had integrated Suzette to its physiology, nor even as large as the one that had consumed Asami. It was about twice as thick as a human, but Caitlin couldn't see how long it was because only part of its body was above ground.

Its mouth opened wide enough to envelop Dallas Tanner. The great worm erupted from the ground with explosive force, punching through the moon's surface with ease as Dallas fell into its mouth, his arms and legs dangling outside.

Then the creature's mouth snapped shut, leaving only the astronaut's limbs protruding. They could still hear Dallas, though, screaming now, pleading for help as he was contorted into bone-breaking positions. Caitlin reached out and punched the creature in the side, but it had little effect. When she saw another worm the same size as the one that had grabbed Dallas homing in on her, she stepped back.

James was still trying to get the rover upright, but now a group of smaller worms plagued his efforts, cascading down on him from the rover itself.

"Forget it, James! We go on foot."

"Are you crazy?"

Caitlin took a precious second to glance toward the Black Sky LEM. She saw a glint of light from its metallic surface. "I see the LEM. C'mon, they'll get us if we stay here. We have to run."

"Dallas?" He turned to look for him but couldn't find him. "What—"

"He's gone. Let's go James, or we're next."

That was all he needed. He saw the spare oxygen canister on the ground next to the rover and snatched it up. Then he stepped up onto one of the rover's roll bars and leapt from it, over a group of creatures. Fortunately for Caitlin, the worm with Dallas in its maw attracted many of the others. They shuffled about as if in competition for the strange new resource.

"Don't leave me! Caitlin! Mr. Burton!" Dallas was still transmitting from his helmet even though he was now entirely contained within the worm's body. Caitlin wondered with a shudder, even as she ran for the opening left when many worms moved to the one that had ingested Dallas, if he was destined to become like Suzette, entwined with this monstrosity; dead, but still alive, or if he would suffer a mercifully quick death like Asami, his helmet crushing under the predator's teeth.

"Caitlin!" Dallas wailed.

She was swamped with dread, a pity beyond words at having to leave him behind, but to stay was without a doubt to end her own life and that of Burton. She almost said goodbye to him, but then stopped. If she said nothing, he might think the worm's body was blocking his transmission and that's why no one replied. She would rather have him think that as his last thought than know that she left him behind. But then she broke out sobbing with the pettiness of her rationale, with the shame of thinking about herself when he was going through such unimaginable Hell.

"I hear you, Caitlin! I can hear you crying!"

"Caitlin let's go!" This from James Burton, who now stood safely, for the time being anyway, beyond the circle of worm-like beasts, beckoning to her with an arm.

"Don't leave me! It's eating me...it's...doing something..." He emitted a strangely piercing scream, laden with emotion.

"Dallas..."

His anguish rang inside her helmet as she trampled over a litter of small worms while she ran to James, who looked ahead toward the Black Sky LEM. "Caitlin, they're still coming for us this way, too!" He began to run back toward her, stopping when he realized they were trapped on both sides—in the direction of either LEM— by the creatures. It looked to him like they might be able to head off toward the crater mountains to the north, but if the worms pushed them too far in that direction they would simply run out of air and die.

Then Dallas' voice pierced the comm channel again. "My air! It ruptured my tank! My—"

All went quiet on the channel, and in a few seconds the frenzy of organisms around the one that had consumed Dallas grew even more hyperactive as the big worm belched out the air from Dallas' suit.

"At least it's over for him now," James said, taking Caitlin's hand. "Let's go, while they're distracted."

He and Caitlin set off in the direction of the Black Sky LEM, easily sidestepping the worms, who now seemed to have no interest in them, wanting only to pile onto the one that had swallowed Dallas. They had been walking for perhaps two minutes when they heard Dallas' voice again.

"Are you still here? Caitlin? James? Don't leave me! I don't know how...oh it hurts so bad...but I'm...still...alive..." He trailed off into a cry of pure agony.

"What the..." James whispered.

Caitlin froze in her tracks. She whispered back, "It's doing what the other one did to Suzette. Making him a part of itself."

"It's *what*?!" Dallas sobbed. "Oh God no...please help me...it hurts! How am I still alive...I can't feel anything except pain..." He choked off into a gut-wrenching scream that went on for some time.

James looked at Caitlin and shook his head while cradling the oxygen can. *What can we do?*

Caitlin, also not wanting to say anything else that would tell Dallas they were going to leave him, pointed toward the Black Sky LEM. Off they walked.

39 | HOOFING IT

Caitlin and James took giant strides across the moon, dodging occasional pothole-like craters that threatened to turn an ankle. The sun was setting now, urging them to pick up the pace lest they still be on EVA at night. They didn't know if the creatures became more or less active after the sun went down, but they knew one thing: if they became any more active it would spell the end for the humans.

They kept a constant eye out for any kind of motion. With no wind or even air to create motion, the moon was a perfectly still environment. Any kind of movement would indicate the presence of the creatures. After a while, the sound of Dallas' tortured screams stopped—whether because he died or they were out of radio range, they didn't know, but hoped for the former.

The pair had gone about a quarter of the distance to the LEM when they came into contact with a new procession of animals. This one was wider than the other they'd seen; less a straight line and more of an advancing horizontal swath.

"Starting to think it wasn't such a good idea to vent the lander." James stopped walking to survey the approaching throng of aliens.

"We'll be glad we did when we get to the other lander." Caitlin hoped this was true, anyway. *Dallas thought it was a good idea, and he was almost always right about everything...* Thoughts of his worm ingestion nearly paralyzed her with anxiety and she forced herself to study the moonscape just ahead—the way to the new lander.

"They're in a wide line but spaced out more," James observed. "Looks like there are gaps we can fit through."

"Remember, they can be underground, too. That's how they got Dallas." She shoved aside the visual of the astronaut falling into ground that opened up like a sinkhole, without warning, without sound, without hope of escape...

"Caitlin! C'mon, stay focused!" The FAA man brought her back to their unpleasant reality. "Where do we try to get through?"

Caitlin scanned the pack of animals that were just ahead and moving toward them. She pointed to a gap in the line off to their left. "Looks like they thin out that way."

The unlikely duo set out toward the advancing phalanx of underground creatures. "Try to tread lightly if you can," Caitlin said, easing a foot to the ground. "They can probably detect the vibrations of our footfalls."

James agreed and also made an effort to be light-footed. Looking off to their right, the line of animals extended all the way into the mountainous crater region, while to the left it thinned out. They continued to skirt around to the left, taking them farther from the LEM in order to avoid a confrontation with the creatures. When they reached an area where they could only see a sparse population of worms, with five-to-ten-foot gaps in between each individual, on the surface, at least, they decided to go for it.

They approached side by side, Caitlin looking to the right and James left. Straight ahead was clear. Behind was clear. Nothing but flat moon. But right and left the soil rippled with activity. As they neared the creatures, they began to run, not wanting to stay in one place for too long and present a target. The mad dash worked. Both of them emerged on the other side of the line unscathed. They didn't stop running, though, wanting to put as much distance between themselves and the animals as possible.

After a few minutes on the move, they paused to evaluate their progress. The line of worms was behind them and they could detect no soil movement ahead of them. The LEM stood in the distance, but closer now, the setting sun beaming off its metallic structure. They trudged on, the novelty of trekking on the moon having somewhat worn thin by now, replaced by the drudgery common to long-distance walking anywhere. Still, they had to keep a sharp eye out for danger, but the lengthy low gravity hike gradually took its toll, sapping their strength.

It was difficult to judge exactly how far away the lander was, and for a while it didn't seem to be getting any closer. Perhaps they were walking around it instead of in a straight line towards it? James mentioned how they should have brought a compass, and

Caitlin explained to him that compasses don't work well on the moon because the strength of its magnetic field is too low. Something Dallas had once explained to her in great detail, but she dared not dredge up those memories now and left it at that.

They were relieved when sometime later they began hearing radio transmissions. At first they assumed they were from the Black Sky LEM, meaning they were close, but as they listened and the transmissions grew clearer, it became apparent they were listening to Mission Control back in New Mexico. Caitlin could barely discern Ray's voice through all the static, but to her it was unmistakable nonetheless, and buoyed her spirits. "Ray? Ray It's Caitlin, you copy me?"

She stopped walking while concentrating on picking out his reply from the noisy signal. She heard the name "Blake" a few times, then "be careful."

"Be careful of what, Ray?"

"...liar... covering things up..."

And that was all they received before the signal was lost.

They pondered Ray's words while they plodded on toward the lander. "Be careful of Blake, he said. Right?" Caitlin asked James.

"I think so. A little late with the warning, unfortunately. Obviously, we all should have been worried before we left, what with his covering up the discovery of life on the moon—and hostile life at that—shortcutting safety procedures. What's worse, according to Stenson, it doesn't seem like this Kennedy fellow is any better. The egos of these rich guys are too big to make room for anything resembling restraint."

Caitlin said nothing but silently agreed. She had failed to see the signs herself, that much was clear to her now. And she had worked for Outer Limits for much longer than James had been involved. It embarrassed her that she had known so little about what Blake was actually doing, so she said nothing, just kept marching toward the LEM that would hopefully be able to get her back home where she could make a fresh start.

Before long, it became obvious they were finally approaching the lunar lander. They scanned the area for signs of the creatures. Thankfully, they saw no processions of worms heading either to or from the ship. The pileup of worms on the side of the LEM, however, was still there. They'd be able to approach the ship without any problem, but they'd have to get closer to see exactly what awaited them.

That's when they heard more chatter from Mission Control. Not Ray at first, but then his voice erupted onto the channel. "Caitlin ...copy?" Static still garbled the transmission.

"I hear you Ray!"

"Caitlin: they're coming... files I found on Strat...deleting before they know..."

Caitlin knew that Blake was inside the Black Sky lander and probably wouldn't be monitoring this frequency. She pressed Ray for more information.

"What's happening? Ray!"

Then they heard signs of a physical struggle playing out nearly a quarter-million miles away. Grunts, heavy impacts, sharp *thwacks...*

The radio signal was cut entirely and they heard no more.

Caitlin looked to James. "My God, something terrible is happening at Mission Control! Ray..."

The FAA man eyed his suit's oxygen gauge and then looked to the LEM's door. "We'll get to the bottom of that and do what we can. But right now, we better get inside. I'm pretty low on oxygen."

40 | PROBLEMS, PROBLEMS

Caitlin made for the LEM's outer airlock door, James Burton close behind. When they were almost there, a monster worm erupted from the ground in front of them. Caitlin sprawled backwards, barely missing its incredible girth. The thing was thicker than the LEM. Not only that, but a contingent of smaller worms came crawling from around the corner of the lander. The airlock was only a few feet away but now entirely blocked by the moon animal.

It was James who had the solution this time. He gripped the oxygen canister—that awkward burden he'd lugged on foot all the way from the rover crash site—and loosened its valve. He pointed it away from the LEM door toward the corner of the ship around which the animals had congregated at the oxygen leak. Then he reached down and extended a hand to Caitlin.

"I let out a little oh-two in that direction." He turned to look. No sooner had he completed his sentence than the gigantic worm submerged again back beneath the soil. The smaller individuals, too, moved off in the direction of the fresh jet of gas.

"Now! Airlock, c'mon." Caitlin jumped the rest of the way to the door and hit the button to open it. It seemed like an agonizingly long time, but in fact was only seconds before it did. She and James rushed inside and she hit the button to bring the outer door down. There was a moment's panic when a smallish animal wriggled beneath the door as it closed, but it cut the creature in two, half of it wriggling autonomously inside the airlock while the other half remained outside.

"We have to get rid of it; kick it back out." James stared at the blue fluid leaking from the severed organism. "I saw what that stuff did to Martin..." He zoned out into his own hellish reliving of a terrible event caused by these strange moon dwellers until Caitlin brought him back, as he had done to her back at the crash site.

"You kick it out, I'll get the door. Opening in three...two...one...now!"

The first thing both of them did was to make sure no animals were lurking just outside the door, waiting to ambush them. But the area immediately outside the airlock was free. Burton swiped the messy half-worm with the side of his foot until it tumbled out onto the regolith. He stamped the smear left behind by its fluids and then wiped the sole of his boot in the soil. Then Caitlin pulled him back inside and hit the button again. They double-checked the airlock before pressing the button to open the inner door that led to the ship. Were they to fail to observe a small creature, it could get inside the ship and wreak havoc later, possibly explode its guts all over them, killing them all.

They looked around for a minute, an easy task since the floor was smooth, white and bare. Still, they were thorough, even checking the walls and ceiling. "I think it's okay." Caitlin placed her hand on the button. James nodded his assent and she opened the inner door. It raised and they walked into the lander's cabin.

They had expected to enter a noisy, hectic environment of engineers collaborating in an argumentative way over how to fix the oxygen leak and other problems. They were surprised to find a quiet, still scene. Only one of the Black Sky astronauts appeared to be working on anything. The rest of the crew, including Blake, Kennedy and the other FAA rep, Stenson, were huddled at a control console, some seated, some standing. None of them were saying anything, they just stared in silence at the two newcomers as they stripped their helmets off.

"What's up?" Caitlin led off, knowing that whatever it was probably wasn't that good, given the cool reception.

Blake rubbed his eyes for a moment before looking up at her. "Caitlin. Mr. Burton. I'm glad to see you made the trip here safely...where's Dallas, still coming in from the airlock? I'll wait for him so I don't have to repeat anything. What I'm about to tell you is of critical importance."

"Dallas didn't make it." Caitlin was surprised at how calm she sounded—and not just sounded, but felt. It was as if she'd already processed the horror of it and now could only mention it in a matter-of-fact way.

"He stayed behind in our lander?" Blake still wasn't getting it. "I hope not, because Arnie, here, sustained an injury while attempting to fix the ship—a mechanical injury, he wasn't attacked by one of the worms—but he needs medical attention."

"There's no Black Sky physician on board?" This from Burton, who eyed his counterpart, Stenson, as he said it.

Stenson gladly took the ball, shaking his head, but it was Caitlin who cut him off, deciding that what she had to say was more important. And it just so happened that it was.

"Dallas is dead. He was eaten by one of the worms on our way over here."

That shut everyone up.

"You're kidding. Tell me you're kidding?" Blake didn't sound like he wanted to hear the answer to his own question.

"No," Caitlin said, while James shook his head.

"How long ago?" Blake asked.

"About two hours ago."

"And you're sure he's dead? It's not possible he was dragged away and then escaped? Or..." He looked down at the floor. "Like Suzette?"

Caitlin made eye contact with each of the group in turn, then slowly nodded. She suppressed a chill as she recalled Dallas still transmitting from inside his vermiform prison. "More like Suzette."

"Jesus..." Blake whispered.

"So we've got no medical doctor," Kennedy said, clearly upset, "which, to be honest, was one of the bigger advantages your team brought to our table, Blake."

"What was your medical plan supposed to be, coming up here with no doctor, anyway?" Blake fired back.

"Each of us is a trained EMT plus we had a videoconferencing app in place."

"So much for that," Burton said, enjoying the grin he elicited from Stenson. In the past, they had had their differences, but they could agree on this much.

"We weren't counting on the dust storm of the century in New Mexico," Kennedy said.

"We weren't counting on a lot of things, either," Blake said.

"Oh?" Kennedy shot back. "It seemed you were counting on life on the moon. You knew these things were up here—"

"Kennedy, please!" Caitlin interrupted. She looked to Blake. "You said you were about to tell us something important. What is it?"

Kennedy had another brief stare-down with Kennedy during which neither man said anything, and then he addressed Caitlin. "Calculations have been run." He paused and looked around at the others who'd been there before Caitlin and James had walked in. None of them had anything to add.

"And?" Caitlin prompted.

"It's clear that this lunar lander, slightly smaller than our own, does not have sufficient fuel supply to get all of us to one of the two orbiting command modules that will make the trip back to Earth." He paused to let this sink in while he stared at James and Caitlin in turn.

James Burton was the first to speak. "Did I just hear you say that this ship doesn't have enough fuel to reach either of the two orbiting command modules? And can it even dock with Outer Limits' module in addition to its own?" Burton looked to Kennedy, who nodded.

"It can. That's not the problem at all. And the ship does have enough fuel to reach a command module, by the way, it just doesn't have enough to bring all of us on board."

"How many pounds are we short by?" Caitlin looked around the group, most of whom averted her gaze, except Kennedy, who answered.

"Equivalent to one person."

"One person won't be able to go back? You're sure about those calculations?" Burton raised his voice.

"We've run the numbers at least half a dozen times," Arnie said from a sitting position that favored his injured leg.

"Triple-checked everything," Black Sky astronaut Jack Williams added. "We made sure all non-essential gear was subtracted for the calculations—anything we could leave behind that isn't needed to get us to the CM. It always comes out the same—not enough fuel with the weight of all of us on board—

barely enough if no errors or unanticipated events occur if we lose the weight of an average person plus their spacesuit."

The group discussed additional combinations of equipment, but in the end it always came back to the same thing: one person had to stay behind or the ship wouldn't make it to a Command Module.

"There's no way to siphon fuel or somehow pick up extra fuel from the Command Module and then use that to bring the lander back down here for the other person?" Caitlin posed, still unwilling to give up.

All of the other astronauts shook their heads until Williams said, "No possible way. That type of transfer mechanism is simply not in place."

"Time's ticking, people," Kennedy reminded them all. "We're burning much needed oxygen and battery power the longer we stay down here."

Caitlin asked to see the calculations one more time and reviewed them carefully. At the end of her inspection, she shook her head and handed back the computer tablet. "It is what it is."

Blake nodded. Kennedy nodded. They all agreed. One person had to be sacrificed in order for the craft to liftoff and be able to reach its rendezvous ship.

41 | DECISIONS, DECISIONS

Kennedy Haig called over to Takeo, who, since returning to the lander, had been working on a tricky assortment of mechanical fixes to the oxygen delivery system. Everyone needed to be present in order to arrive at a course of action. When the entire crew was seated, Kennedy began.

"This is a most uncomfortable situation, for all of us, I'm sure." No one disagreed, and Kennedy continued. "But we do have options, however slim. Let me begin by asking point blank..." He eyed Blake as he said this phrase, "... Is there is anyone among us who would like to volunteer to be left behind?"

Eyes widened and mouths dropped open. James put down his notepad; he knew it annoyed everyone that he still took notes, but he had always performed his job duties no matter what and he wasn't about to stop now. "You mean, do any of us volunteer to die? That's what you're asking, isn't it? The other LEM is non-functional, and this one can't make two trips, so...to stay behind is to die, am I right?"

Kennedy nodded. "That is correct. But the legacy that individual leaves behind will be everlasting and—"

"Cut the crap, Kennedy," Blake said. "Nobody wants to be left behind. Am I right?"

They all nodded, including Kennedy himself.

"As I said, it was merely an option, of which we have few."

"Well, that option stinks," Blake said, to a murmur of agreement.

Kennedy shot him a hard stare. "Very well then, Mr. Garner. As I said there are options, however few and unpalatable they may be. Here is another. Since we have no willing volunteers, I propose that you yourself take the high road and willingly stay behind to leave a lasting legacy, since it is you who is basically responsible for causing this mess in the first place."

Blake got up from his chair and stepped over to Kennedy, their eyes a few inches away. "What are you talking about? You better watch what you say, Kennedy!"

Kennedy shrugged. "You're the one who kept the presence of this hostile alien life form a secret, thereby endangering us all, including yourself and your own crew. And one of your own astronauts—Strat Knowles, whose worm entombed body I laid eyes upon myself—was left behind up here already, so clearly you knew about the threat and tried to cover it up. It would be a form of cosmic justice for you to be left behind now, some might say."

Blake's face turned beet red. "Cosmic justice! What about cosmic justice for the fact that it was your reckless technological shortcutting that endangered your ship and crew, putting myself and my crew in the position of having to come to your aid?" He flailed an arm about the cabin. "This ship was going nowhere if it weren't for the supplies and equipment we provided you with. Therefore, I submit that it should be *you* who is nominated to stay behind."

Kennedy's eyes narrowed. "You always were a shifty, conniving bastard, Blake, you know that? Yeah, you've done well for yourself, no one can deny that. But at what cost, Blake, *at what cost*? Remember all those companies you bought out in the late 80's, early '90s when you were 'cutting your teeth,' as you say, on mergers and acquisitions? All the families you threw into turmoil after you fired all those workers for no good reason other than to assert your power, to let them all know, *this is my company now and I'll do what I want with it*! You stepped up your own ladder created from the broken backs of others, Blake. And now that's what you're looking to do again, isn't it? Someone is going to die here, so that you may live, is that it? Someone, anyone, just as long as it's not you."

"And you weren't doing the same thing along the way, Kennedy? You're not exactly a pauper yourself. You don't get to be a billionaire without stepping on a few toes along the way, that's just how it goes."

"Everything I've done has been with decency and by the guide of a moral compass, which is more than I can say for you. You must think—"

He never finished his sentence because at that moment Blake struck him in the chin with a quick uppercut. The sound of Kennedy's teeth slamming together filled the cabin and then Kennedy lunged at his attacker. The two men grappled with one another in a standing position, legs lashing out in an attempt to trip as well as to kick. Although businessmen with no real fighting experience, both Blake and Kennedy had taken part in various fitness programs over the years, usually with personal trainers, and these included martial arts and kickboxing.

Kennedy's astronauts circled around the fighting billionaires, but it was James Burton who actually stepped in and pushed the two men apart. As soon as he did, the others stepped in and were able to corral the two fighters into opposite corners of the ship, placating them by telling them it wasn't worth it, they had a job to do if they were going to be able to get back to Earth, that they could damage the ship even more, they had to work together...

"Stop it!" Caitlin stepped into the middle of the two men, each now surrounded by a others who held them back. "You're being ridiculous. Now let's get back to work."

"Maybe that's what they were doing." This from Stenson. "They're staging a fight to the death so that we don't have to pick someone to leave behind. Is that it, *gentlemen*?" he placed sarcastic emphasis on the last word.

"No." Blake shot Stenson a withering stare. "Just making a point."

"You're an idiot, Blake," Kennedy called out. He was immediately shushed down by his astronauts.

"Everybody listen up!" Kennedy shoved off his minders. "It's clear that none of us are going to volunteer to stay behind. That's fine. I was just asking. No one is going to be tricked or forced into it." He paused to look each of them in the eyes, with the exception of Blake.

"Then what are we going to do?" Caitlin asked.

"There's only one thing *to* do," Kennedy said. "We hold a lottery."

42 | DO YOU WANT TO PLAY A GAME?

The entire crew sat on the floor in a circle with their legs crossed, "Indian style," Caitlin thought of it, reminding herself of her grade school days. She had no idea why it was called that, but right now that was the least of her worries. Whoever lost this game of chance was going to die. On the moon. As alone as a human could possibly be.

"What can we use for straws?" Kennedy asked.

Takeo moved to another part of the cabin. "I'll look for something in the hardware bin over here."

Kennedy nodded. "I think we probably have a length of spare wire over there that we can cut up into different lengths."

Blake snorted. "*Spare* wire? I didn't think we had spare anything on this ship."

Kennedy shot him an angry glance. "Apparently we have a little more to spare than your ship, which is why you're here."

Blake's retort was cut off by Caitlin putting a hand on his shoulder, a silent reminder to calm down, now is not the time to start another fight. Blake still seemed like he was about to keep at it though, and Caitlin was glad when Takeo returned to the group carrying a length of electrical wire in one hand and a pair of cutters in the other. He handed both off to Kennedy, who looked around at the group, counting heads aloud.

"...eight. So we'll need eight straws." He held out the wire as if considering it. It was yellow, about two feet long. Blake picked up the wire cutters.

Caitlin stared at the wire. "If we assume that length of wire is thirty inches, then the average length of each straw should be..." She stared up at the ceiling while calculating in her head. "... Three point seven five inches, so one of them has to be significantly shorter than that."

Kennedy nodded as he eyeballed the wire, held in his left hand. Then he put it between the cutter's blades, moving it left to right before coming to a stop almost four inches from one end. He made the cut and the first straw fell to the floor in front of him. Everyone looked at it while he moved the wire along the cutters again, this time snipping off another four-inch length.

All eyes watched as Kennedy lined up the first two straws he'd made so far on the floor in front of him. Then he returned to his cutting, snipping off more pieces of wire to make the next five straws. He set down the cutters and then proceeded to line up the five new straws next to the first two, the eyes of those present still watching his every move. He then brought the remaining strand of wire to the cutters again. "Now to make the short one."

He clipped off a three-inch length and held it up for the group to see before placing it on the end of the row with the others. He pushed them into place so that the ends were exactly aligned, the short straw easily apparent. He looked up at the group, the hum of air handlers and various electronics the only noise.

"Here we go." Kennedy gathered the straws until they were all clutched in his right hand. He used his left to carefully pat down the tops until they were all even. None of the straws protruded below his clenched fist. He stood and held out his hand with the straws.

"Are there any objections to me holding the straws? If so, any of you may volunteer." A few glances were exchanged but no one said anything. "Statistically, there is no advantage or disadvantage to holding the straws," Kennedy reminded them, or informed them, as the case may be for the non-astronauts who were not as mathematically adept. "If I'm holding the straws and all of the long ones are picked first, then I lose."

James Burton appeared confused, or at least highly concerned. "But for those drawing in later rounds, they have fewer straws to choose from, increasing the odds that they'll pick the short straw, right?"

Kennedy and the astronauts, including Caitlin, shook their heads. She explained it to Burton. "That risk is equally compensated for by the chance that someone who draws before you will pull the short one." There were no further disagreements about this and so Kennedy proceeded.

"Now then... In case you're not sure of the rules," he said with a smile, "a different person picks a single straw until the short one is pulled. That person is the loser..." He appeared to think better of that choice of words and paused while he rephrased his statement. "...that person loses the game, I should say." No one said anything. They all stared at his hand with the straws.

"Why don't we go clockwise around the circle?" He looked at Caitlin, who stood immediately to his right. She took a deep breath and reached her hand out toward the straws. She inserted two fingers into the tight circle of wires and plucked one out. Her knees nearly buckled with relief as she heard someone mutter the word, "safe," and she realized she had not drawn the shortest straw. *I won't be left behind to be ingested by those things...*

Kennedy wasted no time and looked next to Arnie. The injured astronaut extended his hand almost eagerly, as though he was competing for a chance to win a baked good at a raffle instead of a one-in-eight (one-in-seven, now, everyone knew) chance at death.

"Wait a minute." James Burton raised his hand like a kid in a classroom. Kennedy's eyes glared at him. "What is it, Mr. Burton?"

"If one of the astronauts loses, are we still going to have sufficient expertise to fly the spacecraft back to Earth?"

It was a fair question, everyone knew it, but Kennedy acted as though it was the silliest thing someone could ask. "Of course! It's not ideal, but then this entire situation is far less than ideal, am I right? Our astronauts can do each other's jobs in a pinch. Correct me if I'm wrong." He looked at the astronauts.

The professional spacemen –and woman—appeared uncomfortable as they eyed one another. Perhaps there was an unspoken communication in those looks: *If we say, No, our jobs are too specialized, then we're all safe!* But whether out of sheer honesty or professional pride (*we're astronauts, we can do anything!*), that's not what they said.

Arnie addressed Kennedy. "Depending on who it is...if one of us loses...that person might have to provide some specialized training, but it could be done, to be fair, sir."

Kennedy nodded. "Thank you for confirming what most of us already knew." He glanced at James Burton, who shrugged. He was looking forward to his retirement, and if he thought of something that seemed like it could affect the likelihood of his getting to live it out, he was going to say something, reactions be damned. Kennedy went on.

"Now...where were we? Ah yes..." He extended his hand to Arnie. "Draw, please."

Kennedy's employee reached out without delay and pulled a straw from his boss' fist, eyes bulging as he examined its length.

"Not the short straw," Kennedy said, his voice level.

Stenson was next. Kennedy held his hand out to the Black Sky FAA rep, who, perhaps subconsciously, recoiled, his hand shrinking back from Kennedy's. "C'mon, Mr. Stenson, dragging it out doesn't make it any better. Let's get it over with. Please."

"All right. I thought I was going out of turn for a second, is all. I'm ready." His hand shook as he brought it toward the remaining straws. Kennedy held his fist rock steady in the air. Stenson hovered his fingertips over it. He dropped them down, only to raise them back up again, then plunged them into the lot. He quickly yanked his hand back clutching the selected straw, then slowed his movements so that he could see the results of his actions. His hand froze in mid-air as his mouth dropped agape. He rolled the little piece of wire between his fingers and flipped it this way and that in his hand, but it didn't change the fact that he had drawn the short straw.

The cabin was silent as all of them gawked at the short piece of wire in Stenson's still unmoving hand. He had lost the game.

He had lost his life.

Stenson snapped out of it, jerking his head up to look at Kennedy, who still maintained his closed fist held out in front of him. "Let me see the rest of them."

A simple request, but one that carried with it so much weight. Kennedy turned his hand palm up and opened his fist, revealing the four remaining wires of obviously equal length. Stenson stepped forward, eyes widening as his gaze bored into the long wires, the symbolic straws that meant life over death. "They're not lined up evenly. Let me see them lined up."

One of the astronauts put a hand gently on Stenson's shoulder and said something meant to be soothing that was not audible to the wider group. Kennedy's reply was matter-of-fact.

"I'm afraid you drew the short straw, Mr. Stenson. Lay it on the floor, here, and I'll show you."

Stenson dropped the wire so fast it was like it was burning a hole in his hand. He eyed Kennedy's hand with the long wires as he eagerly waited for them to land next to the one he'd chosen, so he could see beyond a shadow of a doubt that he had in fact picked the shortest straw. Maybe he hadn't, after all. Maybe it just looked like the shortest one because of some trick of the light and he would be vindicated... But Kennedy shook his head at Stenson, as if reading his mind, pitying his delaying of the inevitable, extending his hand to let the five wires fall to the floor.

Just as Stenson started to rail about wanting to see the other two straws—the ones picked by Caitlin and Arnie before him—a sixth wire dropped from Kennedy's hand to the floor next to the others.

"Wait a minute!" James Burton said, inching closer to the pile of wires on the cabin floor. "Why are there seven wires on the floor?" He looked at Caitlin and the Black Sky astronaut who had already drawn. Both of them still had their chosen straws in their hands.

"You still have yours?"

They nodded, adding them to the collection on the floor, where the cut lengths of wire now totaled nine, even though there were only eight people. The extra wire was the same length as the other long ones. It was dropped with the other five, the unchosen ones, from Kennedy's hand. The attention shifted to the Black Sky CEO, who looked to the floor and back up to meet Burton's intense gaze.

The entire group stared transfixed at the anomaly until Burton spoke.

"You saw me count them out for you on the floor and pick them up into my hand," Kennedy said.

Blake pointed at the pile of straws that numbered one too many. "Then how did the extra long one get there?"

Kennedy stared at the five straws without an answer.

"Let's see the other two!" The condemned man seized on the anomaly as a glimmer of hope. Caitlin and Arnie both placed their wire straws on the floor beside the existing row of six, including the short one drawn by Stenson.

"So that's all eight straws accounted for—seven long plus one short—except that there's also one too many longs. A total of eight longs and one short!"Blake turned his gaze back to Kennedy, who still stared at the floor. Blake looked his rival carefully up and down.

"None of us ever came into contact with that wire, with the exception of him." He pointed to Takeo, who had given Kennedy the wire. The astronaut shrugged and nodded at Kennedy.

"Yes, I brought him the original length of uncut wire."

Burton's eyes were also fixed on Kennedy. "He did bring him the wire but he never touched it after it was measured—its length estimated, at least—by Caitlin." The female astronaut nodded to corroborate this. Burton went on.

"We all watched Kennedy cut the wire." Everyone agreed, including Kennedy himself, who appeared unsure where Burton was leading.

"So somehow either the wire was longer than we thought— maybe it was bent, doubled back on itself where he made the cut, creating two pieces?"

Again, Kennedy was in agreement, nodding his head vigorously. "It's possible. I was calculating how long each wire had to be, I wasn't really looking at the wire itself that closely..."

"Or..." Burton said. But he didn't have to complete his own sentence.

"You cheated!" Blake yelled, pointing directly at Kennedy.

Suddenly, the entire space capsule rocked to one side and they heard a deafening noise from above.

43 | HOUSE RULES

Kennedy puffed out his chest, indignant, while everyone else looked up at the ceiling. Something scrabbled around up there, outside, something on top of their craft. James Burton was first to break the silence.

"One of those animals got up there somehow."

Caitlin traced the being's progress across the ceiling. "We've got to get it down before it causes damage. Everything's barely working as it is; we can't have any more malfunctions."

"Pardon me, Blake? What were you insinuating?" Kennedy ignored this new threat, focusing instead on confronting Blake.

Blake's face went through several shades of red as he prepared to level his accusation, but it was Caitlin who said something next, her carotid arteries bulging as she got her point across. "Are you two *listening*? We need to do something about that damn worm or worms up there right now, or forget about choosing one of us to die up here, we *all* die."

At this, Kennedy raised his voice. "Only one of us is going to die, and that's Mr. Stenson, because he lost the game. Fair and square!"

But Blake argued back, causing Caitlin to abandon her attempts at reason with the two leaders and to turn to the others. "Listen! Listen to me!" she screamed. That did the trick and bought her the entire team's attention except for the two CEOs, who continued to yell at one another. Caitlin pointed up through the roof. "In a few minutes, our Command Module will pass overhead in lunar orbit. If we miss this pass then we'll have to wait hours for the next rendezvous opportunity, while the creatures attack the ship. I'm not sure we'd last that long, so we need to do what we have to do to liftoff right now."

All but Kennedy and Blake took this to heart. Even Stenson, who only minutes ago wasn't even sure he'd be alive to worry about it. While Caitlin huddled in conference with the others to discuss how to rid the craft of the creatures so that they would have a chance of making the rendezvous with the Command Module, Blake addressed Kennedy.

"You're the one who came up with the idea to draw straws. Or wanted us to believe you came up with it on the spur of the moment, I suspect is more accurate. I think you knew all along that's what you were going to do. You were even the one who suggested using a piece of wire to make the straws! Which means that you had time to snip off a piece and stick it up your sleeve *before* we gathered to have the meeting and draw the straws."

"That's preposterous! I did nothing of the sort. I don't know how that piece got there. Maybe *you* anticipated the game and smuggled in your own straw. Could that be it, Blake? You've been accused of cheating before, as we all know. Remember the SensorSoft deal, Blake..."

A crashing noise interrupted all conversation, a reminder that the creatures still rampaged around the ship and with every passing second the possibility of irreversible damage multiplied. Caitlin pointed and Williams donned his spacesuit helmet in preparation for leaving the ship to do something about the worms.

Kennedy glanced over. "You're going outside? Good, take Mr. Stenson with you, please. It's time. Pete, I'm terribly sorry, but—"

"I don't think so!" Stenson yelled. "You cheated!"

Blake took a step toward Kennedy. "Cheating means you lost."

"Mr. Stenson lost."

"You lost, Kennedy! You cheated, you forfeit by default! You stay behind!"

"Absolutely!" Stenson chimed in. "I will not volunteer to be summarily executed when the integrity of the game has been called into question."

Blake beamed at this. "It's you, Kenn—"

He never finished his sentence because at that moment Kennedy's fist slammed into Blake's nose, breaking it. Blake staggered in place but managed to remain on his feet as a gush of blood sluiced down his face.

Realizing he'd been injured and wishing to prevent it from happening again, Blake reached down, unclipped his spacesuit helmet from his belt and put it on, fastening it down in a surprisingly quick and smooth motion. But Kennedy, aware that his blows to the head would now be rendered ineffective, did the same. The two fighters now stood a few feet apart, fists raised, facing off in their impromptu armor.

Blake swung first in this new round, a left cross that glanced off Kennedy's space-suited chest. The Black Sky CEO reacted with a strike of his own, landing a jab to Blake's midsection.

At that moment, Williams came running back inside and took off his helmet. He brandished some type of blowtorch. "There was a huge one crawling around up there. Gave it a little incentive..." He held up the torch. "...and it scooted off. Those things have formed almost a complete ring around us. They're maintaining some distance...for now...but I wouldn't count on it lasting for long."

"Doesn't matter," Caitlin said, moving to a bank of controls where she carefully eyed a display. "If we don't lift off in the next five minutes, we're stuck down here for another..." She paused while examining a different screen. "Ten hours and forty-four minutes."

Another astronaut shook his head. "Our oh-two won't make it that long. The ride up to the Command Module is only about an hour if we hit it on this pass. That we have oxygen for. But ten hours..." He trailed off as if imagining all of them suffocating together in the ship.

"Then let's move." Caitlin's hands flew over the controls, but the other astronauts simply stood there watching the fight play out between Kennedy and Blake, who now circled one another, trading jabs and even the occasional kick.

Burton made a move to come between them and break it up, but caught an errant elbow to the temple and backed off.

"Forget them!" Caitlin said, turning around from the console but leaving her hands in position on the knobs. "Activate the launch systems, let's go!"

"One person has to get off or the ship will *not* make the rendezvous with the CM," Takeo reminded.

Caitlin fired back a reply without delay. "It takes five minutes to initiate the launch sequence. We need to start the process now or it won't matter who's going or not going because we'll have missed the rendezvous."

The fight escalated, with Kennedy and Blake clinching, arms around one another, until Kennedy shoved his opponent toward the astronauts. They caught him, preventing him from slamming into the wall, but Kennedy was charging, head down like a bull. The astronauts scattered, leaving Blake standing there alone. The Outer Limits CEO sidestepped Kennedy at the last second and it was Kennedy's turn to stumble forward, until he collided with the same wall he had intended for Blake.

They heard the thrum of electronic systems activity and Caitlin spun around. She picked up her suit helmet with two hands, about to put it on. "Thirty seconds until we *have* to leave. Suits on, everyone."

"Someone has to get off!" one of the astronauts screamed just before he donned his helmet and secured his suit.

"Not me!" Stenson shouted, cowering back from the astronauts, further away from the ship's airlock. He pointed at Kennedy. "He cheated. I played fair. I'm not losing my life to a cheater. I'll fight! I will fight any of you who try to throw me out! Rip your fucking suits!" He suddenly produced a box cutter, razor blade extended as he waved it around.

Blake and Kennedy began trading blows again, avoiding the helmets in favor of random body blows. They careened about the ship, the fight getting wilder, more out of control. Caitlin knew it wouldn't be long before they broke something critical, but even that wasn't her main concern anymore.

She shouted at the top of her lungs.

"Initiating liftoff! Someone leaves or we all die."

Kennedy swung a hard right cross at Williams, who tried to come between him and Blake. The astronaut backed away after the fist grazed his chest, tripping and falling onto the floor. Kennedy went back to his pursuit of Blake, who stood his ground when he could but was being slowly pushed back as he dodged multiple blows.

"Do something, now!" Caitlin wailed.

James Burton, who had been silently watching the battle play out from his place against the wall, prepared to move as Blake was backed up toward him by the advancing Kennedy. As Burton started to move, he brushed against the airlock switch, which had a safety cover that had already been opened. The inner airlock door slid open, although no one seemed to notice. Caitlin still yelled that they were going to miss the rendezvous, and the astronauts still tried to break up the fight. Stenson continued to cower far from the airlock, box cutter in hand while his gaze darted nervously about.

And then Burton saw his opportunity. He wasn't sure what came over him, how he knew that this was what he must do, but something inside him hinted it was the only way. He slid along the wall away from the now open inner airlock door. Kennedy threw a powerhouse left at Blake's stomach, but missed, his fist connecting instead with the doorframe. He howled in pain while Blake jumped on his hunched over form, knocking him to the floor. Around them they heard the rumbling, industrial sounds of the spacecraft preparing for its ascent into lunar orbit.

The two fighters rolled on the floor into the airlock, the battle having gone to the ground. They were wrestlers now, wearing spacesuit costumes. The other astronauts, seeing the chance to physically contain the belligerent men now that they were on the floor, started to rush into the airlock. But Burton's hand lashed out onto the button and the door slid shut before anyone else could enter the transitory space.

"What are you doing?" one of them breathed at Burton.

"You heard Caitlin. We have to go. Those two don't want to go, then fine. Let them stay here."

Burton heard a gasp from someone but he didn't care. No one protested, either, as his hand moved to the button that controlled the outer airlock door, the one that led directly out onto the moon, into space. He clicked the button and the outer airlock door opened.

The two billionaires were locked in embrace by the outer entrance, continuing to grapple with one another as the outer door opened. Then Blake executed a decisive and forceful move, hurting Kennedy but sending both of them tumbling outside in the process.

Burton hit the button inside the airlock to close the outer door.

44 | YOU BOTH LOSE

The two fighters stopped brawling to look up at the ship. The outer airlock door was closing. Blake scrambled up and started to run for the door first, but he was too late, the door sealed before he could slide a boot under it. Inside the LEM, James flipped a switch to disable the outer door control.

Kennedy smacked the airlock door button on the outside of the ship, then hit it harder when that had no effect. Blake and Kennedy began transmitting from their helmet radios, shouting at the crew to open the door.

James ran from the airlock back into the ship and hit the button for the inner door, closing it also. The astronauts stood watching him, unsure of what to do. He turned to face them.

"What else can we do? Caitlin says we need to leave or we all die."

Her voice confirmed Burton's statement. "Ignition sequence in ten...nine...eight..."

No one said anything, but no one did anything, either. Kennedy's and Blake's voices could be heard over the rumbling of the rocket engine as it prepared to liftoff.

"Only one person needs to be left behind! It's Kennedy, not me—I'm still out here! Let me in..."

Caitlin directed the other astronauts to man their stations. Then she spoke to Blake. "I warned both of you, we had to leave. We still may not even make it back ourselves. There is nothing we can do. I'm sorry, Blake and Kennedy, but you two have brought this upon yourselves. Good luck and peace be with you. You will be remembered."

"You can't do this! This is murder!" Kennedy yelled into his helmet radio. He and Blake backed away from the ship's exhaust plume, no longer fighting as they watched their ride home prepare to depart without them.

"Being the first humans to die on the moon will ensure your legacies will never be forgotten," Williams pointed out.

"Where is your compassion?" Blake asked.

Caitlin's voice answered them amidst the intense thunder of the liftoff engine. "...and liftoff!"

The lunar module rose from the moon's surface. James looked out of the small window to see the two CEOs staring up at him, their differences finally forgotten. He didn't know if they were aware of it yet, but a thick ring of the creatures surrounded them, waiting for the liftoff exhaust to clear. Already they were moving closer, James could see. A couple of huge, tanker truck-sized individuals lumbered among them. He couldn't help but wonder if soon Blake and Kennedy would be embedded into one of those large organisms, taken on an everlasting tour of the moon...

Ahead in the Command Module, Paul Abbott prepared for docking with the lunar lander as the mixed but now united crew stared in awe at the magnificent, humbling earthrise filling their windows. James Burton left the window and strapped himself into a seat, the closest one to Caitlin, who sat in what would have been Dallas' position in the pilot's seat. She adjusted the radio to the frequency that would call Outer Limits' Mission Control and asked if anyone copied. After a few seconds, her face lit up as she heard Ray's voice coming in much clearer than it had been for the last transmission.

"Oh my god! Mission Control to Outer Limits, we copy you loud and clear! Caitlin?"

"It's me, Ray, it's me!"

"What the Hell happened? The telemetry we're getting shows that the LEM is out of oxygen completely! We thought you were...I thought..." His voice broke as he imagined the unthinkable.

"It's okay, Ray. Our LEM is out of oxygen, but we're not in it. We're in Black Sky's LEM. Their Mission Control should be patching through to you any second to establish communications for the rest of the flight."

"Copy that! The dust storm is clearing here on the ground. You should be okay to land by the time you get here in a couple of days, over."

"Roger that, Ray. I'm coming home, baby." Caitlin clicked off and turned her attention back to the flight controls. Then, after a brief technical chat with Paul in the orbiter, she turned her attention to the view outside. James Burton also marveled at it, in an almost trance-like state.

"Beautiful, isn't it?" she said to him.

Burton nodded as he stared at the Earth, growing slowly larger in their window. "It is, but I'm starting to think it's a lot more beautiful from the ground."

THE END

www.ingramcontent.com/pod-product-compliance
Lightning Source LLC
Chambersburg PA
CBHW032000170626
46807CB00006B/2569